I0731122

A TOUCH OF DARK

PAINTED SIN BOOK 1

LANA SKY

A Touch of Dark

A Touch of Dark By Lana Sky

Copyright © 2019 by Lana Sky
All rights reserved.

No part of this publication may be reproduced, distributed, or transmitted in any form or by any means, including photocopying, recording, or other electronic or mechanical methods, without the prior written permission of the author.

This is a work of fiction. Names, characters, businesses, places, events and incidents are either the products of the author's imagination or used in a fictitious manner. Any resemblance to actual persons, living or dead, or actual events is purely coincidental.

Cover Design by Charity Chimni
Editing by Mickey Reed Editing
Formatting by Charity Chimni
Proofreading by Charity Chimni

ONE

he bigger they are, the harder they fall.

I hate that stupid saying, but sometimes it's the only one that fits—poetic justice, in a sense. My father used to be a monolithic figure in this city, a giant in his own right. But then he fell pretty damn hard, inspiring a million cliched headlines.

Ex-Judge Under Fire.

Racial Bias Suspected in Overturned Murder Conviction.

Today's doozy read: **Killer Vindicated?**

Some asshole brought a stack of the latest tabloids to the office and left them in the damn boardroom. To provoke me? Torment me? No matter the reason, any other day, I'd do the daughterly thing and burn them all.

Unfortunately, it's already pushing midnight, and I was able to sequester myself in my office only a few minutes ago.

Locked behind the frosted glass door, the fake smile I've been sporting for hours falls flat.

Tonight, my father's drama has to take a backseat for once. What was that line he always spouted?

A man is only as strong as the cracks in his mask.

He loved uttering that one from the bench more than any other saying. As one of the harshest judges in the state, he excelled at peeling back the façades of those in his courtroom and revealing the monsters lurking underneath: Criminal. Liar. Sociopath.

Until now.

Overnight, he's gone from hero to hypocrite and his advice doesn't feel so warranted anymore. Some people wear masks for a fucking reason.

Mainly to hide behind.

Nerves creep down my spine as I finally feel along the wall for the light switch while looking everywhere but at my desk. Alone, I can't suppress what is so easy to hide around a room full of analysts hanging on my every word. None of them suspected what this day truly means to me—at least apart from the "I'm a workaholic" cliché.

How had Sharla from accounting put it? "You must be the only woman in the world who loves when stuffy meetings derail her birthday plans, Ms. Thorne. Like, seriously."

She had a point. The date on the calendar is an ominous reminder: I can't avoid my present forever.

Happy birthday to you.

That awful tune echoes in my mind as I face my desk and spot the beautiful gift someone left beside my computer monitor. A rectangular box wrapped in black paper and topped with an ebony bow.

I know that security footage or the guard downstairs will refute the suspicion that anyone came into my office while I was gone, but there is no erasing *his* presence. My nostrils flare, catching the familiar scent of sweat and cologne, and a grim sense of nostalgia washes over me.

Happy birthday to you.

I flatten my hand against my hip to stop from reaching for the phone. No. I don't need to call my therapist tonight. I'm a big girl. According to that fucking book she made me read, "mentally healthy" people can find the positive in any situation. Think happy thoughts and such.

Like, there will only be ten death threats waiting on my office voicemail once I gather the nerve to check. There's a positive. Score one for optimism.

You and your whole racist family can go fuck yourselves.

I hope you get raped like that Borgetta whore, you bitch.

I'm sure they'd love your daddy in prison.

The insults serve as a fitting soundtrack as I unwrap my present. Surprise. Like every year, I've received a bottle of vintage wine—but it's the thought that counts. Keeping in the spirit of optimism, I choke down my customary sip.

Three years of receiving the same brand and I'll never get over the bitter taste. Or the name of the vintage, printed in red on a black label: *Enduring Tradition.*

I continue to sip as I run my fingers over the ebony business card the bottle came with—but I wait until my breathing steadies before flipping the card over. White font forms a simple message:

To another year. — Simon

My hand shakes as I pour more wine into a two-dollar mug scavenged from a drawer. It has a smiley face on the front, beneath the headline: *You're never lonely with a...*

I contort my mouth while eyeing my reflection in the floor-to-ceiling windows across from my desk. The woman staring back at me looks regal in her black Versace cocktail dress—a congratulatory present to myself that I now regret. The wine is worth more.

Adding insult to injury, I look exhausted despite the smile. Nothing like the beaming, prize-winning marketer gazing from the framed photo behind me. To be fair, she's a creation achievable only with the finest coating of makeup and tweaking in photoshop. Juliana Thorne is her name, and I barely know her.

A paragraph-long blurb on the company's website reveals all anyone needs to understand anyway. Selling lies is her one talent, and her résumé is the only interesting thing about her—that and her coveted last name.

Sighing, I set my mug aside. I've wasted enough time. Simon needs his answer after all.

I open another drawer and withdraw a blank postcard before grabbing a pen from the neat row beside my keyboard.

I'm fine. To prove it, I inhale deeply and drag the nib of a pen across the page. It only shakes twice. *To another year,* I write as neatly as I can.

With that, the celebration commences. I swipe my desk clean and tuck the postcard into the pocket of the black coat hanging on a hook behind my office door. Then I sling it over my arm and step out into the hallway that attaches my office to the main suite.

I'm the only one left behind, as per usual. The janitor already switched the lights off, saving me the trouble of having to lock up. So I toss my postcard, addressed only by name, into the outgoing mailbag and then take the elevator to the main lobby. Gus, the security guard, is lounging against his podium, flicking through a skin mag. He looks up at me and winks as I slip past him.

"Happy birthday, girlie," he says. Then he frowns. "Everything all right, Ms. Thorne?"

"Everything's fine."

"Good. I hope you aren't paying attention to the news, either. We all know that beaner got what he deserved. He killed that girl. Your father just had the guts to prosecute. It's not his fault he offed himself, is it?"

When I don't reply, he continues. "I mean, a man like your dad can't have an evil bone in his body, taking in a traumatized little girl out of the goodness of his heart—"

"Goodnight, Gus!" I force a smile before leaving the building, forsaking the heat for the frigid night air.

Outside, my grin falls flat as that mental tune starts up again, building in time with my surging heartbeat. There isn't enough room in my skull to care about my father's legal issues and the narrative being spun around him.

Happy birthday to you… Happy birthday to you.

I grit my teeth to refocus. A town car is already waiting for me out front. The driver appears by my side to usher me inside, and I'm left with only a blurred view of the city to distract me.

That and the chatter of a radio station coincidentally discussing the one topic that seems to be the talk of the town.

"That judge should be stripped of his title," a presenter says. "They only convicted the kid because he was an immigrant—"

"Not just any immigrant though," someone interrupts. "That 'kid' came from a family that isn't exactly innocent. Say what you will, but the Villas have their fingers in some shady stuff. Everyone knows it. But hell, if I wind up in a river tomorrow, we know why—"

"Could you turn that down?" I ask the driver, who complies.

But as silence falls, I quickly realize my mistake when my thoughts turn to what I know is waiting for me at the end of this short trip.

Simon always sends two presents. One goes to the office, which I'll have to open in a public setting. The second comes to my home address—which he manages to find despite how many hotels, motels, or high-rise condos I've rented, booked, or hidden in. The past three years, I've stopped trying to evade him and maintained the same sublet penthouse of a luxury hotel in the heart of downtown. It boasts the highest standard of security around, with cameras in all the halls and guards on twenty-four-hour patrols. I even paid extra for a private floor.

Regardless, like every year, I find a neatly wrapped box waiting before my door.

I stoop for it and unlock my door, knowing that, just like at my office, the guard down below will deny letting anyone up and a review of the cameras will show nothing. After so many years, the fear gripping my chest has become reflexive at this point.

Morbid tradition.

After stepping inside the suite, I cross the foyer and head straight for my bedroom, switching on every light I pass. The gift under my arm feels more familiar than the modern apartment with its open floorplan and gray color scheme. In a sick way, he became my fixture, Simon. No matter what, I could always count on him.

We will always play our game.

Tonight, I set the gift on the edge of my bed and fish a bottle of wine from under the mattress first. My toes curl shamefully. *Coward.* This brand is cheaper than the stuff he sent me and burns going down. I chug right from the bottle until my stomach aches and the world spins around me, a merry-go-round of monochrome. Only now do I sink to the floor and wrestle the gift onto my lap.

Happy, happy birthday.

He chose red wrapping paper, like always. *Her* favorite color. I run my fingers over the surface of it. Malicious intent lingers in the neatly folded corners and carefully applied pieces of tape. He selected the color of the bow, too. It's a deep, rich shade of purple. *My* favorite.

Details like that mattered to children the most. A favorite color, betrayed by a shirt or backpack, could spark a friendship over lunch with few words spoken. It was a craft you could hone to a T if you knew what to look for. The loner girl lurking around the edges, shuffling her brand-new shoes in the hopes they'd be noticed by someone. Anyone.

A good monster could prey on that weakness and turn anxiety into trust. I used to excel at it.

Enough reminiscing. A forced exhale can't ease the tension seizing my lungs as I unwind the ribbon and lift the lid.

Swaths of white tissue paper shield the objects inside. The first is a newspaper clipping. **Local Girl Missing** proclaims the headline. In the body of the article, the writer went straight to the point. *Seven-year-old Leslie Matoda disappeared shortly after four p.m. on October 28th…*

I stop reading. The article slips from my fingers and the wine bottle replaces it. Two hard pulls and the resulting dizziness almost erase the guilt searing a hole through my stomach. Almost. Squeezing my eyes shut can't block out the memories, however.

Naked trees formed a silent audience as he placed the knife to her throat.

"Now remember," he warned. "Simon says play…"

I gulp down more red liquid. Less clarity. Dizzy. Dizzier. It's no use. Terror crawls up my throat like bile until my mouth opens and only noise comes out. High-pitched and broken.

Damn it.

I'm *not* breaking. I'm practicing. My therapist is a fan of therapeutic screaming. "Try it into your pillow," she likes to suggest every other session. "I think you'll benefit from a cathartic release, Juliana."

Bullshit. Screaming couldn't help me then and it doesn't help me now. Not when smothered into my white duvet or muffled behind my hands. Crying doesn't, either. Or shouting.

It's only when I stumble into the bathroom and plow my fist into the mirror—sending glass shattering over the sink —that I finally feel something. Icy numbness followed by burning, stinging pain as drops of ruby-red moisture splatter my white color scheme.

But it's not punishment enough.

I slam my bleeding, aching hands onto the counters so hard they throb. Bruise. I kick dents into the cabinet doors and rip the gray shower curtain from the rail. It's still not enough.

It never is.

Neither is reentering my bedroom, yanking all the beautiful, expensive clothing from my closet, and tossing the pieces onto the floor. Or shoving my mattress from the frame. Breaking glass. Throwing objects. Smashing. Destroying. Obliterating.

I run out of steam near the foyer and only have enough energy left to topple the glass grandfather clock that guards the entrance to my suite. With a monstrous roar, it smashes to pieces, much like everything else in my life at the moment.

Happy birthday to me...

And many more.

TWO

I never get drunk. What in college was a fun quirk now feels like a curse. Or perhaps a biological defect inherited from my birth father. The man couldn't bother to remember my birthday, but he gave me a gift that keeps on giving: I can drink to my heart's content without ever blacking out. It helps that my stash of wine makes for a delicious diversion while providing no reprieve from the horrors I desperately seek escape from.

As Daddy would call it, *quite the conundrum.*

If only I weren't too much of a coward to move on to another vice. I'd give anything to finally utilize the prescription the new therapist wrote weeks ago, shoved inside my nightstand drawer. Maybe peace lurks within a different bottle? Bite-sized calm at a grand a pop?

As it stands now, I have nothing but five lamps in this room alone, turned to their highest settings, to combat the dark.

Thunderstorms worsen the onslaught of flashbacks. Like the storm I sense now, rumbling in the distance. The air is too still. Ebony clouds swirl along the horizon before the stillness breaks with a monstrous roar of thunder.

The taste of copper burned my tongue. I couldn't spit it out. He was behind me, prowling over the underbrush like a living shadow, impossible to outrun.

Guttural and low, his voice chased me. "Come out, come out, Juliana..."

Wait. A girlish bit of laughter doesn't belong in this memory. The images of the forest fade and I'm in my apartment again, gasping for air.

Despite this being a private, residential floor, the odd intruder isn't too uncommon. Most people wonder what it's like to live here in the Lariat Hotel, in the proverbial lap of luxury.

All they have to do is ask me and I'd tell them.

It's a charming, gilded prison.

The voices, one male and the other a giggling woman, draw me from my fetal position. I leave bloody streaks as I cling to the wall for balance and look out through the peephole. Two intruders wander the hall, both wearing cheaply made party clothes. I have toilet paper worth more than this girl's dress. Soft, bright pink, no expert tailoring in sight.

Her voice, breathy and high-pitched, sounds distorted through the door—but it's not Simon's, so I strain my ears to pick up every nuance. "I think we're lost." She giggles while leading her male friend by the hand. He keeps pulling on the sleeves of his oversized suit jacket but copies her manic, pixie grin.

"You just want to get back to that freak, don't you?" he teases. "Maybe we can get him to paint you like that. Naked and shit—"

"Knock it off!" She strikes him playfully on the shoulder, and they disappear down the corner, leaving laughter behind like breadcrumbs.

Freak? Painting? Naked?

The thread of a mystery entices me more than continuing my birthday celebrations. For now. Some Band-Aids and a pair of gloves disguise my bleeding cuts. For added armor, I slip my winter coat on and I've almost reassembled my façade.

Almost.

A glance in the mirror hanging near the door reveals the dreadful state of my makeup. God, I look awful, my eyeliner smeared and my lipstick faded. Sighing, I swipe it off and salvage what I can beneath a stern expression.

I never cry. I'm the woman who conquers the world with a frown and a mild shade of red lipstick. But bloodshot eyes give me away now. I see myself for what I really am: a fraud. A pretender. A goddamn murderer.

Stop it. I catch my bottom lip between my teeth and bite down hard enough to chase the thought away. Then I scramble for the door and enter the hall as thunder snarls. There's no sign of the couple, their trail of laughter now cold. I'm forced to chase their scent. Cheap perfume. Cloying cologne. I follow the smells to the set of elevators on the other end of the hall and take one down to the lobby.

I usually avoid this entrance. Guests and visitors alike flood in through glass doors at all hours. It's noisy and loud—kryptonite to my nerves. Tonight, the atmosphere feels even more electrified than usual. A glance ahead reveals why. A crowd swells beyond the lobby doors, held back by the hotel's security. Blurred faces jockey for space along the glass, illuminated by intermittent camera flashes. Reporters. For me? Daddy's house has been swarmed for months, but no one has bothered me yet.

My palms start to sweat, which irritates the open cuts, and breathing takes more focus. Ironically, there's a remedy for the anxiety nearby: the lobby bar directly to my left. Oh, the promise of more wine. Merlot makes for a tempting diversion, but something else catches my attention before I can claim a stool for myself.

Misery loves company, and I'm not the only one having a shitty night.

"How was I supposed to know?" a woman hisses into a cell phone. Hunched against the wall, she draws notice anyway, being tall, blond, and dressed to the nines in a black suit. Clutched in her free hand is a clipboard she's waving through the air like a shield against guilt.

"Look. I had no idea he'd be this pissed off. I saw the address on some documents in his studio and they had amazing rates and—" She purses her red lips. "No. It's too late to change it now. I think he's on his way. I have to go."

She hangs up and crosses the reception hall to stand near an archway that has a sign propped on an easel beside it. The real reason behind the sudden increase in publicity? The hotel sometimes hosts events open to the public. In fact, I've booked a few for clients of mine here and there. Book signings. Galas.

A Window into the Soul this advert reads, red font printed over a black backdrop. *Displaying the art of Sampson.* I'd recommend the design to my own clients: It's simple but bold enough to draw the eye to the artist's name.

Sampson. I've never heard of him, though I appear to be in the minority. People are waiting in a sizeable line to enter the ballroom, craning their necks for a glimpse through the doorway.

"Miss?" The woman with the clipboard watches me expectantly from the distance of a four-person gap. I've wandered into the line without realizing. "Do you have a ticket?"

I shake my head, and she nods.

"Don't worry. Sampson appreciates every guest, and we always offer vouchers at the door. I just need your name."

"Juliana Thorne," I say, stepping forward. "What exactly is this…"

My gaze cuts toward the doorway behind the woman and whatever else I meant to say dies in my throat. I'm vaguely aware that I'm still moving, drawn forward like a moth to a flame.

The portrait hanging from the wall ahead is a woman composed of ivory, lying contorted on a bed of blood-red roses, her eyes unseeing, her hands grasping at nothing. Etched with incredible care, she looks livelier than the person I see whenever I look in a mirror.

Woefully alive and yet painfully dead.

The artist didn't spare an ounce of detail. Every wayward hair, pimple, birthmark, and scar of his subject is on display in stark clarity.

"Incredible, isn't it?" someone exclaims beside me.

"W-what?" I blink as the rest of the world returns one jarring realization at a time. For starters, I'm standing in the back of the ballroom, nearly nose-to-nose with a painting hanging from the wall. A sheet of glass separates me from it and displays my reflection.

Wide-eyed. Mouth agape. Pupils dilated. Red lips that quirk into a frown. I've never seen this look on my face before. I take my time trying to pin down just what it might be but fail to come up with a single term.

"Here, you forgot to take this."

A glossy brochure makes its way into my hands courtesy of the blond woman who worked the door.

She catches me staring and winks. "I felt the same way the first time I saw one of his works. Enjoy." She scurries off, leaving me to survey the rest of the gallery alone.

Twenty women join the first, trapped in their own worlds of darkness and roses. Observed together, they rip me from the elegant setting, dragging me into each brutal scene. Flowers. Passion. Death. Those are the recurring themes.

I'm no art connoisseur, but I can recognize talent—and this artist oozes it in every brushstroke, along with a million other tiny details. Such as his indifference to his subjects. The cruel attention given to the fear lurking in those blank irises. The cold, twisted elegance of lifeless limbs.

Each portrait pulls me in before I'm swept along to the next. Far too soon, I find myself before the first painting again, unable to toe the respectful distance every other spectator keeps. Curiosity yanks me closer against my will, step by step.

Finally, I reach out with a trembling finger—

Commotion.

I turn and find a gaggle of people huddling together in the center of the ballroom, jockeying for a glimpse of someone: a man whose sheer presence urges people from his path. Literally. The crowd parts like the Red Sea.

"It's him," I see a woman mouth to her companion, wide-eyed.

Him. The lone unaffected figure, I presume. A man who takes my breath away—the same way walking outside, butt-ass naked in the dead of winter would.

Suddenly and lethally.

My father is—was—a judge, and I'm more than used to imposing men. We had politicians who controlled the livelihoods of the entire state over for breakfast. I lived in the mayoral mansion for three years. Summered with the governor's children.

Neither Daddy nor those in his orbit ever commanded a room as this man does. And for that, I count my blessings. Simon is terrifying enough to live in the shadow of—and he's just a shadow.

This man is darkness. He stands tall, wearing black almost from head to toe: a tailored suit that screams of old money and careful taste—and brawn. The ebony material strains over broad shoulders and muscular forearms.

Trailing my gaze upward, I expect a face worthy of the intrigue, but he's like one of these paintings: a mixture of handsome and strange. A stern jaw anchors what I can only assume are Romanesque features, mingled with a hint of the exotic, though a dark blindfold obscures most of them, hiding his eyes. It's tied neatly over the bulk of a black ponytail that reaches down to his shoulders.

Such a strange accessory, though it doesn't appear to hinder his confident stride.

"I can't believe it's him in the flesh," a woman nearby whispers. "He doesn't look like a kingpin."

Is he a celebrity of some kind? Or maybe the artist himself? I browse the brochure in my grip, but it only contains representations of the paintings, never their creator.

When I look up again, he's holding court in the back corner of the ballroom as men in black suits stand guard nearby, intimidating the crowd from coming too close. Beside the blindfolded man is the blond woman. Her gaze cuts in my direction as her lips move rapidly near his ear.

I turn back to the painting and try to shut the rest of the world out again. It's surprisingly easy to, the longer I stare. No need for pills or booze. Just soulless eyes formed from intricate strokes of paint.

The woman could be me in the right lighting. Therefore, she's the perfect canvas to project all my flaws onto. Alive, I bet she wore Versace and hated her birthday.

I bet she hated herself.

The longer I stare, the uncannier the resemblance seems. Am I seeing more of my reflection than the art? I brush my fingers against the glass, but I can't decipher what's paint and what's reflection.

"Do not touch, *por favor*." The deep voice accompanies the hand seizing my wrist without warning.

I shiver and whirl around. Then my brain stalls, spitting out a few disjointed thoughts before total malfunction. *Handsome. Dark. Up close.*

"The glass is fragile," the blindfold-wearing man warns. His voice is deeper than I expected by looking at him. Suave, grated tones fall like off-notes from a piano. Jarringly out of place.

"Sorry," I croak, wrenching my hand back. My heart races, surging beneath my skin. Strange. I press my fingers there, counting each frantic beat. Thump. Thump. Thump. "S-sorry," I repeat.

His jaw tightens in an elegant display of rippling muscle. "You need to leave."

"I...I'm sorry?" People are staring. Probably at me: openmouthed, my cheeks flaming. "I didn't mean—"

"I'll have my men escort you out." He nods, beckoning one of the stern-faced bouncers closer.

"W-wait."

Just leave, Juliana, a part of me urges. I have a birthday to conclude. Screams to smother. Dealing with some conceited prick should be an easy headache to tick off my to-do list. Or not.

"Are you the artist?" I ask.

At the sound of my voice, he grits his teeth. A silent denial? Or grudging acknowledgment?

"I…I'm interested in buying. I think."

"Are you even familiar with the artist's work?" A droll quality laces his tone. Amusement? No, something darker that makes me quiver in my heels before I can help it: hostility.

Another "admirer" of my family, perhaps? I bite my lip and resist the urge to kick myself for not taking Daddy's advice to hire a bodyguard. To be fair, my reasoning made sense at the time. Why pay for someone who would always prove ineffective against the real monster?

"Are you?"

My cheeks heat when I realize I still haven't answered him. "No," I say. "I've actually never heard of him until tonight."

"Oh?" He runs the edge of his thumb along his chin. I can't shake the feeling that the act draws attention to his face on purpose. Again, I suspect he knows me as more than just a story from the tabloids. But I don't know him. "And your thoughts?"

The change in subject is enough to give me whiplash. "Well…" I return my attention to the painting. Nice would be the polite word—or something along those lines. Something to strike up a conversation around. Any other day, I'd know what to say. Tonight, I'm filter-less. "I think…I think it's terrible."

"Terrible?" The man laughs. "How so?"

"I…" I shrug, once again compelled toward honesty. "Not in a bad way."

"This isn't the place for you." His warm breath heats my earlobe and chills me to the core, making me jump. "I suggest you leave. Now."

"Why?" I counter, surprised by how irritated I sound. "If you recognize me from the news, I'm not drawing attention to myself."

"If?" he wonders, his tone dangerously soft. "Perhaps you've recognized me from the 'news'?"

"No." I feel like I've missed something. Maybe he is a celebrity—some pompous prick with his head so far up his ass that he can't stand not being recognized. "I think I'd remember you," I say.

A shadow flickers over the glass in front of me as I sense him looming over my position from behind. He smells strange up this close. My flared nostrils gobble up the scent but I can't place it.

"One would think *you* would."

I know he's gone without having to turn around, but the aftermath of his tone ricochets through me. I should do what he said: leave. But before I can take a step, my gaze returns to the painting and I'm riveted once more. It's as if the woman's dead stare perfectly sees through everything I try to hide and, unlike the rest of the world, she gives it to me straight.

You'll never fit in.

"Excuse me, miss."

The blond woman from the door yanks me from my reverie for the second time. She's lost her clipboard, clutching a stack of brochures in her hands instead.

"I'll leave in a minute," I insist.

"Oh, but I'm sorry. The gallery is closing." She gestures behind her. Sure enough, the crowd has dissipated. I'm the only guest remaining.

"Oh."

A tendril of anxiety gnaws away at the lining of my stomach. No, not yet. Five more minutes. Or maybe longer.

"How much is this one?" The question is out before I can reel it back in.

Impulsivity. It's one of the many traits my therapist urged me to work on. Acting on impulse led me to alcohol. Bad decisions. Oopsies. Mistakes.

"How much?" The woman blinks. "I-I'm not sure, but Mr. Sampson's work has sold in the tens of thousands before—"

"What about twenty?"

"I-I don't—"

"Fifty, then." I step closer to the painting, leaving her to decide on an answer, even as I reach into my pocket for my checkbook.

Odd. This painting makes for the first birthday present I've wanted in years. One dark enough to rival even Simon's grim offerings.

Happy birthday to me.

THREE

Come out, come out, Juliana...

I bolt upright, drenched in a cold sweat as my eyes fly open to my empty room, and the icy noose of fear loosens with the realization that I'm alone. It was just a bad dream, though Simon wasn't the nightmarish figure who chased me awake this time.

No. My pursuer sported a blindfold, his motives a mystery but his hatred more electric than the flashes of lightning greeting me from beyond my window.

An omen?

Or a reminder. Simon's days of gift giving aren't over yet. He always allows me twenty-four hours in between our games, but no more.

Usually, I'd spend that time stocking up on wine, but I'm forced to oversee the cleaning crew tasked with reassembling the shambles of my apartment first. They fix my bedframe and repair the damage to my closet, assembling the clothes in the correct color-coded order. One benefit of using the same company every year is that the workers know my preferences—but they never ask questions. I pay extra to ensure that.

I also order them to avoid the bathroom. For now, anyway.

Afterward, I catch up on a bit of work and find a message on my cell phone from Heyworth Thorne. *See you tonight, sweetie.*

Every year, he humors just one request, a truce of sorts: We forsake dinner on my actual birthday, but the night after, he insists.

How he loves to show me off. Perfect little Juliana: the traumatized brat he took in out of kindness and turned into an upstanding citizen. Presto! Like magic.

Love makes it easier to withstand the lying, but never the guilt. God, I wish I could be that person for him. The perfect daughter. I try. I've tried. But being her is like wearing a pretty dress. After a while, it itches. The material wears away at the seams. It tears.

Until it isn't so beautiful anymore.

Tonight, my disguise will be a black Vera Wang paired with something navy. Hmmm. I scour the glass display case along the back wall and hunt for a fitting necklace. The sapphire Daddy gave me a few years ago will do.

With my costume all picked out, I linger in the living room and watch the world waste away down below. The real estate agent referred to this view as "to die for." Maybe she's right. Three years spent where Simon can easily find me and one glance from the window makes the torment almost worth it.

I can watch people play out their lives from this height without them ever being the wiser. That woman walking her poodle has performed the same routine for two hundred and seventy-two days in a row. There are no calls from Simon to disrupt her charming façade. No. It's the scruffy man she lets creep into her house late at night when only the glow of passing traffic can illuminate him.

They do their song and dance day in and day out, but she never forgets to wear her pretty smile in the aftermath.

I practice mine in the reflection on the window. Wide, but not too wide.

I almost fool myself.

A sudden knock on the door interrupts my practice and a frown flutters across my lips, displacing my hard-earned expression. But then I remember.

Giddy. That's the only way to describe the bubbling sensation building in the pit of my stomach as I pad across the foyer and answer the door.

The blond woman from the gallery stands on the other end of it. She's exchanged the pantsuit for a gray skirt-and-blouse combo.

"Ms. Thorne?"

I nod, and she steps aside, revealing a man behind her pushing something long and square balanced on a utility cart.

"I took the liberty of accepting your bid on Mr. Sampson's behalf," the woman explains. "Were you still interested in the painting?"

"Yes." I lurch out of the way, allowing them inside.

Due to disposal limitations, the earlier cleaners left the glass shards of my grandfather clock in a bin near the door for later pickup, though I had them wipe the blood from the walls, at least. The woman eyes the mess before directing her attention to the empty wall adjacent to the floor-to-ceiling windows. Prime real-estate for a morbid portrait, apparently.

"Here?"

I agree and the worker snaps to attention. He removes a plastic covering, revealing the painting. When viewed in the overcast daylight filtering into the room, it looks grislier than it did last night. Ghostly and harrowing. I suck in an appreciative breath and write the fifty grand off as money well spent.

Once the painting is mounted, my one regret is not buying a matching frame for it. Encased only in a covering of protective glass, it looks far too delicate against my muted design scheme.

"Mr. Sampson appreciates your patronage," the woman says once I've signed the final document she shoved beneath my nose. "I'll let you in on a secret: He donates most of the proceeds to charity anyway. Though I have to say that not everyone appreciates his work."

"Oh?" I bite back the words that spring to my tongue. *No wonder.* If he treats every prospective buyer like he did me, I can imagine why.

"I'm surprised you haven't asked about him," she adds, an eyebrow raised. "No offense, but the few who do buy the paintings—and they all are mostly women—tend to use the sale as a foothold to pry. 'Are all the stories true?'" She mimics how I assume she thinks a socialite with thousands of dollars to spend on a painting sounds. "I will say I'm impressed. I think that's why I'm even here in the first place. He rarely offers a painting for sale, but hopefully he won't mind. At least you won't try to hound him for a date. To some women, he's more myth than reality now."

I picture the mysterious figure from last night and shrug. "I know what it's like to have people pry into my life. Sometimes, the intrigue is better than the reality."

"Fair enough," the woman says, but I can tell she's still bemused as I escort her out.

Alone, I finish another cup of coffee and find myself gazing at the painting, desperate to decipher the secrets lurking beneath every layer of paint.

Sampson. I've never heard of him—and in this city, anonymity only extends to those who don't matter at all or those who matter too much. Privacy is a commodity even I can't afford.

I'm tempted to look him up. Try my hand at Google. A part of me doesn't want to, however. Maybe that's the fun of it all. The allure. My first ever birthday present to myself in over twenty years and I don't even know who made it for me. Or why. Or what possessed him to blend death with flowers. Beauty with horror.

Or why he seems to despise me.

I'll never find out.

And unlike my dealings with Simon, I don't have to.

FOUR

A town car arrives for me at six on the dot. After cajoling the driver into taking the long route to the suburbs, I spend a majority of the ride silently rehearsing my lines in a compact mirror.

Hello, Daddy. Pause and smile. *I've been fine.* Blink. *You look wonderful, and so does Diane.* Flash an even bigger smile, and then the finale, uttered with a mischievous tilt of my head. *Will there be cake?*

It's the same script I've recited at every other birthday dinner, and he never demands more—only that I show up and let him have this one day. A handful of hours when we both can pretend that my past doesn't matter.

I owe him that much.

Determined to put on the best performance, I pour all my energy into arranging my flawless outfit and perfecting that easy, confident smile. I'm ready by the time the driver turns onto the long driveway leading to the secluded, astronomical-acre plot Daddy bought the moment he retired.

Squaring my shoulders, I exit the car and put my rehearsed steps into motion. Smile first. Confident walk. The moment I mount the first stone step leading to the door, it opens from the inside as if on cue.

And my stomach drops right to my stiletto heels.

Daddy is wearing that tired gray suit from his glory days and a pinched expression. No warm smile. No arms outstretched for our customary hug. Instead, he ushers me inside with a wave of his hand. "Welcome home, sweet pea."

I follow him uneasily. The house doesn't feel the same despite the cheery coat of yellow paint brightening the entryway. Something's wrong. A subtle tinge in the air renders everything out of place. Odd. Off. The feeling grows as we enter the private study—not the dining room down the hall, where I know everyone else is waiting, poised to shout "Surprise!" on sight.

Glimpsed from the side, my father's expression is as stern as it used to be when he was on the bench and nearly jumped out of his skin every time someone said "boo" to me.

"Juliana…" He sighs, and a telling sent wafts from his breath. Tobacco.

I raise an eyebrow. "Have you been smoking?"

"That doesn't matter." Concern weighs his weathered features down, exaggerating the wrinkles around his eyes and his mouth. He looks so old today.

Maybe I look older. I can't tell in the reflection staring back at me from the glass case displaying various legal paraphernalia. My face is transposed over one of his many awards. How fitting. I'm part woman. Part trophy.

"Juliana?"

"I'm fine—"

"You look tired." He smooths a wayward lock of hair away from my face. "Is it the storms?"

Storms. His subtle way of skirting around the dangerous topic we never mention directly: the past.

"We're in the middle of a particularly violent system according to the newscasters, sweet pea," he adds. "Maybe you should sleep here until it passes? Diane's kept the white noise machine you used to use, and there's spare Zofran in the medicine cabinet—"

"I'm fine," I lie. "They don't even bother me anymore."

"That's good…" His hand settles over my shoulder, imparting the comfort and vulnerability only he can.

Like always, I'm a child again around him. Heyworth Thorne, my hero. He saved me when I was only eight years old, from more than just a psychopath. He's tried his best to dust off my cracks and piece my broken mind together.

I smile hard to let him know that he has—force of habit.

But, this time, he doesn't smile back.

"There's something else, darling," he begins cautiously. "I know you won't agree, so I'll just come right out and say it. I want to put a guard on you. Full time. It's just for a little while and I'll ensure they stay out of sight."

"What?" My pretty little mask slips. Over twenty years of secrets. Have I blown the game already? "Why?"

I push past him and brace my hands on the desk to keep standing. Ice solidifies in my veins, choking the air from my lungs. I force in a breath and let it out. In. Out.

"I didn't mean to scare you." He closes the door to his office and comes to my side to dab at my dry eyes with a handkerchief. Another force of habit.

If we can't perform our charming father-daughter routine, we fall into the only other roles we know how to play. Protector and victim.

"It's just… There's a threat," he says. "Against me, but there's no reason to believe that this person won't attempt to target you."

"Target me?" I don't say the obvious: as if they haven't already. But the phrasing means he isn't referring to Simon. Someone new perhaps. "Who?" I ask, steeling myself for the answer.

These days, most of the city is out for Thorne blood. My gaze lands over the newspaper on his desk, and sure enough, emblazoned on the front page is a quote from a legal analyst on the Borgetta ruling: *"Any man tasked with upholding the law should do his due diligence to ensure that no bias affects his ruling. In this case, the bias is clear: Mathias Villa was doomed for nothing more than the color of his skin."*

I stop reading, surprised to discover that it isn't the only topic to make the headlines. A glossy photo of the Lariat ballroom gleams beneath a row of text reading **Reclusive Artist Dazzles at First Public Showing.**

"Don't read that trash." Daddy snatches up the paper and tosses it into the wastebasket. Before I can question it, he forces a grin. "And let's not talk about the nitty details now. It's your special night. Did you enjoy yesterday?"

I nod. Strange. The motion doesn't feel like lying. "I did. I even bought myself a present."

"A present?" He cocks his head. "That does sound like a good day. What did you buy?"

"A painting." In some ways, I'm still riveted by the piece. Pale flesh intertwined with ruby red. Stark violence and beautiful irony.

Heyworth Thorne most likely wouldn't approve.

"A painting," he mutters while fiddling with his tie. He did the same thing the night his first wife died and he tried to explain to a fifteen-year-old me how accidental overdoses happened. "It's almost funny that you'd mention something like that…" He sighs again, more heavily this time.

I gently touch his shoulder. "Daddy?"

He's never looked *this* tired. This old. "Have you heard of someone named Damien Villa?"

"I don't think so." Though the name does ring a bell, I'm not sure why. No face comes to mind anyway.

"You should have," Daddy snaps, a hard note in his voice. "I told you: You need to be more attentive. Especially where that godforsaken place is concerned." He jerks his head in the general direction of the city and scoffs. "Damien Villa is the head of one of the cruelest crime syndicates on this side of the country. *La Muerte*."

All I can do is feign interest while he watches me expectantly. "That sounds intimidating."

"Try murderous," he replies. "They work as the American arm for a Colombian cartel, though he's supposedly reformed. Some say his brother runs it still. He's a monster and a goddamn madman, but because he has enough money to throw around, he's making trouble for me where it matters."

"Are you okay?" It isn't like him to curse. Or glare so harshly that the vein in his forehead lurches against his skin. "Is he threatening you?"

"Ha! At least then I could do something about it," he snaps. "The bastard is too clever to do that, at least not outright. But...he's not above planting rumors. Some of them may even pertain to you, and if you hear anything—anything at all—you must promise to come to me first—"

"Why?" I take a step toward him, but he hunches his shoulders away from me. "Is this about..."

His sigh is unwilling confirmation. On principle, we've rarely broached the topic of the Borgetta murder case, but in the tumult of information spilling through the airwaves, I've heard enough to last a lifetime.

The details are foggy, but I remember the gist: a woman, Emily Borgetta, daughter of a prominent politician, was brutally raped and murdered by a man with ties to organized crime. Daddy threw the book at him: life served in the cruelest prison in the state. Ten years later, a lack of evidence allowed some appeals court to not only overturn his conviction, but declare him innocent—but a few weeks before the final decision went public, the man killed himself in prison. Now, everyone in the world is a legal analyst, the most ignorant of them claiming racial bias in the original judgment. Most spectators settle for calling my father incompetent. Or evil. Whichever looks better in a headline.

After he spent nearly a lifetime on the bench, this case has become a black stain on an otherwise glowing record—and it's killing him.

"I'm asking again: Did he threaten you?" Now doesn't feel like the right time to mention my own log of menacing voicemails. "We could always go public. Do a news conference."

"No." Daddy clenches his fists so hard that his knuckles whiten. "Oh, he wouldn't give me the satisfaction. That sick bastard—" He cuts himself off and meets my gaze directly. "He's dangerous, Juliana. Especially now. And as for a news conference… I haven't told you before, but I've decided to run again, despite these disgusting allegations. I'm announcing it officially at a press conference soon, and I want you to be there. I need you to be there."

I digest the news in silence and wind up observing my hands. They shake. Flattening them against the desk's surface can't disguise it.

After five long years, it's fitting that Heyworth Thorne would choose now, of all times, to jump back into the fray and defend his name. The dread knotting in my stomach is more selfish than anything. Whenever he campaigns, his surveillance of me becomes obsessive. Not that increased patrols have ever stopped Simon before.

But no. It's more than that. An uneasy Daddy means more questions. More covert calls to my therapist to ensure I'm complying with my sessions. The return of his surprise visits to my apartment to discreetly check that I don't have wine stockpiled in the fridge.

He loves me.

He loves his reputation more.

"Don't worry, Daddy," I say, sweetly uttering my expected line. "I'll be fine."

"I'm still getting you a bodyguard." His hardened expression warns I won't be able to change his mind with a bat of my eyelashes. "You won't even know he's there. So don't hold too big of a grudge, eh?" He props my chin against the pad of his thumb and contorts his lips into what passes for a smile. "Now what do you say we get this evening started right? Diane made your cake."

I nod, and we exit his office. It's only on our way through the foyer that I remember what sparked the morbid turn in our conversation in the first place.

"Damien Villa," I start as Daddy waves off someone peeking around the corner who quickly scurries out of sight. "What does he have to do with painting?"

"He owns a gallery," Daddy says, slowing his steps. We're close enough to the dining room to hear the muffled commotion coming from within. Eight people I suspect. The same mixture of family, friends, and neighbors who attend every year. "The police suspect it's how he launders a majority of his money. He's used the prestige and other so-called legitimate business ventures to amass enough political sway to pressure my old donors."

"Why?" I ask. "What does he have against you?"

"Don't worry about him." Daddy takes my hand and gives it an impatient tug. "I'll tell you another day, sweet pea. For now, how about we make this night something to remember?"

I recognize the tremor in his voice. He's pleading, and the scared, desperate little girl I used to be rears her ugly head.

Keeping him happy means smiling on cue.

Maintaining the façade.

Being perfect, darling, wonderful Juliana.

"Sure, Daddy." I beam and step around him, my script at the ready. "You look wonderful, by the way. And you said Diane made cake? Oh, how considerate."

At last, he returns my grin with one of his own, and arm in arm, we enter the dining room to shouts of "Surprise!" The biggest one of all being how my smile doesn't slip once, even as my mental clock continuously tracks the passage of time.

Tick. Tock.

FIVE

I'd kill someone with my bare hands for a glass of wine. Just one. From the good, cheap bottle tucked behind my headboard, preferably. Daddy wouldn't approve, but hell, I've earned his love tonight.

Like the best daughter, I simpered and charmed and had the most "wonderful" not-birthday birthday dinner in existence.

But I'm not ready to receive my next gift.

Lost in my thoughts, I didn't have the sense to request that the driver take the usual detour, so we've arrived at the Lariat way too soon.

Too early.

Simon prefers for me to stumble across his presents rather than lie in wait. A glance at my watch draws a sigh from my lips. Way too early. There's at least an hour to kill.

As I step out onto the curb, I consider the bar. It beckons me from beyond a glittering row of windows. Oh, the promise of salty, stale, expensive wine.

On my way into the lobby I notice that the poster advertising the art of Sampson is still there. A steady line of people streams in and out at the discretion of the blond woman with her trademark clipboard.

She spots me from across the lobby and smiles. "Couldn't stay away?"

Maybe not. The distraction promised by wine isn't as appealing as the cruel honesty of death and floral arrangements, apparently. I'm slipping into the crowd of eager voyeurs before I know it. An unseen figure presses another brochure into my hands, but nothing holds my attention for long—apart from the maze of canvases.

Sampson likes his subjects nude. And it seems he never paints the same woman twice. They all stare from various angles, wide-eyed and contorted in some grotesque pose. Despite the myriad of differences, one feature always appears in every single portrait: pink lips, slightly parted. A knowing, petulant pout.

As if every muse relished her master's attention, right down to the final stroke.

"I thought I'd find you here."

I recognize the crisp voice of the blond woman. I turn to face her, realizing that, once again, I'm left staring long after the thick of the crowd has dissipated.

"I don't do this often," she says before I can apologize, "and I must say that Sampson isn't very fond of humoring admirers. But, as his manager, I'll take the liberty of schmoozing anyone willing to buy. I'm Carla, by the way."

She presses something against my palm. A business card, black and sleek with a glossy finish. Déjà vu strikes like a lance and I nearly drop it. It's so similar to Simon's calling card…

This font, however, is industrial silver. The address printed on one side is presumably Sampson's base of operations.

"I can't guarantee a meeting in person," the woman warns. "But I won't exactly turn you away if you'd like to look at his more…obscure collection."

"Oh?"

Her mischievous wink ignites my curiosity. What pieces might a man like this deem too distasteful for the public eye? My chest tightens at the thought. From disgust? Or anticipation? I'm not in a hurry to decide.

Instead, I finger the card's glossy front before slipping it inside my pocket. If I call a town car now, it would be roughly a ten-minute trip, delaying my opening of Simon's gift just a little longer.

But would the delay be worth it?

I can't settle on an answer during the short trip back to the lobby. The usual crush of people has dispersed, leaving just a few tenants and visitors milling about. This time of year, everyone wears some variation of a heavy coat, disguising the bulk of their features. Could one of them be Simon concealing my present beneath the winter layers?

I'd never know. He prefers to haunt me from afar, always watching. It's his elusiveness that makes him so terrifying, especially back then...

"Are you okay, miss?" A hand brushes my shoulder, belonging to a security guard.

I nod and have no choice but to enter the elevator to keep up the façade.

I'm okay.

At least I am during the silent ride to my floor. Then the elevator doors part and my ruse slips once I find an empty hall, no wayward visitors in sight.

No distraction.

Slow, heavy steps carry me to my door. My palms sweat inside their gloves, which aggravates the healing scrapes. I shake them firmly in a vain attempt to dispel the nervous energy. When that fails, I lie to myself. *You're ready.*

Or not.

As I round the corner, my eyes fixate on the glossy numbers on my door first before roving downward...

And settle on my gray welcome mat.

Five seconds of searching pass before I finally accept that it's empty.

My stomach churns, wrestling with the remains of overly sweet cake and non-alcoholic champagne. How I hate surprises. For the first time in years, Simon's late. Either that or he's settled on a new spot to leave my first gift of the night. Inside? I take my time fishing my keys from my pocket, but the door budges at the slightest touch, already opened a hairline crack.

I shove my hand into my pocket for my cell phone, but I can't explain what makes me push the door open wider without calling 911. Yet.

The light switch lurks just beyond my reach, but I don't flip it. I have a visitor, it seems, who prefers the darkness over the typical introduction: his scent gives him away. Spicy. Masculine. Wrong.

Daddy doesn't smell like this.

Neither do the doormen or usual security guards.

Neither does Simon.

My new intruder's cologne itches like pepper among an amalgam of different scents: shaving cream, rich liquor, and the faintest hint of sweat.

I should call the police, anything but call out, "Who are you?"

"*Buenas noches.*" The raspy baritone is the most alarming attribute of all. It reaches out to me from the living room, carrying a thick accent. "Do come in. Don't mind the intrusion—and I wouldn't call the police if I were you." The warning comes as my thumb twitches against my phone's touchscreen. "They tend to be so easy to corrupt."

"There…there are armed guards downstairs," I croak.

His answering laugh is a slap to the face. "Again," he continues, "easily bought off, Ms. Thorne. Even your father's reputation can only go so far. Come in. Have a seat. I merely want to talk. This shouldn't take long."

His mention of my father triggers a cold suspicion. Perhaps his warning wasn't for nothing. I'm in the living room before I know it, rounding the leather chaise to find a man sitting on it. Alarmingly massive, he transforms the spacious room into a claustrophobic prison. Yellow lights from nearby buildings give vague definition to his frame: a strong jawline veiled by the shadow of long, black hair neatly tied back into a ponytail. The outline of a blindfold, worn even now, stands out in stark contrast to his skin.

I should have recognized him from his voice alone. The man from the gallery.

And suddenly so much makes sense.

"Are you… You're Damien Villa," I rasp. My stab in the dark lands more accurately than I'd like. Another bit of laughter is my reward, decidedly colder than before.

"Ah, *perdóname*," he murmurs. "The innocent daughter of Judge Thorne turns out to be not so innocent after all. And I was inclined to give you the benefit of the doubt, Juliana."

"What do you want?" I take a step back, aware of the fact that the door is still open behind me.

"To talk," he says.

"Talk? You mean use me to threaten Heyworth Thorne? Go ahead. You can try. Then get the hell out." My callous laugh rings hollow. I sound weak, not brave. Tired and pathetic. "I'm sick of you goddamn people wanting to hold him accountable for one goddamn mistake—"

"Ah, *perdóname*, but you misunderstand." His voice contains the same qualities as lightning. Biting. Stinging. Raw. "My current visit has nothing to do with your father, Juliana. This is about an entirely personal matter."

Personal?

"The painting you bought," he continues before I can question. "I ask that you return it. That wasn't meant for you."

My painting. I crane my neck and spot the rough outline of my new possession. The morbid hues feed off what little light there is, creating a ghoulish effect: glowing, dead eyes staring directly into mine.

"I bought it," I say. Though the reminder might be for myself more than him. I bought it. I own it. Mine.

"Oh, but that was a mistake," Damien murmurs with chilling insistence. "On your part. It was never for sale, especially not to the likes of you. Return it to me and I shall overlook this…insult."

"Insult?" I cross the room, observing the painting in all its gory, disturbing detail. The artist's intentions elude me still —cloaked in layers of color and shades of mystery. "How could what I think insult you? Unless...you're Sampson." It's not a question. In a way, I'm stating something I probably already knew.

A madman isn't content to just let his show be displayed unseen. No. He must watch the people watching. He must gauge the full effect. Terror and disgust form the icing on his masterpiece, and he doesn't feel complete without a taste of it.

"The painting belongs to me," he says, evading the subject of his identity. "I'll make the arrangements to have it returned—"

"No. It's mine." I look back at him to watch my words register. "You can't have it."

"Oh?" He stares ahead through the fabric of his blindfold, seemingly transfixed by the view beyond my windows. "Should I take something of yours, then, as retribution?"

My body jolts at the sound of his voice, reacting without permission. Daddy had a pit bull once. Danger was his name. Every now and again, while dozing peacefully by the fireplace, Danger would suddenly startle awake and bark at the shadows. Daddy would shout at him to quiet down, but the beast only settled when whatever unseen threat he'd sensed diminished.

My nerves feel like that now. Humming with awareness of an ominous presence my eyes refuse to register.

"Are you threatening me?" I manage to ask.

"Negotiating," he retorts. "Despite whatever you think of me…I won't have my art used as a pawn, if you please."

"What I think?" Laughing, I shake my head. "I don't even know you."

"But I know *you*, and I know your family. Tell me: Did you enjoy strolling into my exhibition, aware of all eyes on you?"

He's implying something, though I'm not sure what. Something obscene, I think. Cruel.

"I live here," I point out. "Why shouldn't I attend an event held in my fucking lobby? And why hate me?" I add before he can get a word in edgewise. "I am not my father."

"Ah… But you think like him. So entitled to that which was never yours to claim."

Few men could speak the way he does and pack quite the same punch. A criminal, Daddy said. Funny, because this man sounds like a judge, someone accustomed to handing down punishments for any perceived snub.

"I'll return your money in full, of course."

"Keep it." Knowing that its supposed creator now sits behind me, I perceive the portrait from a different angle.

The woman's slight, desperate pout makes more sense. Paired with the unmistakable attractiveness of Damien, her final fate feels all the more tragic.

"So is it true that you use these to launder money?" I sound so disappointed. Though what a stupid question. Of course the art is a gimmick. "Do you?"

Silence lingers between us, forcing me to come up with my own answers. I always did my research when it came to the people in my orbits. Clients. Friends. Possible dates. I learned the hard way that it's better to suspect someone's potential motives from the outset—not that it's hard. The average person tends to fit into the same few categories like a book, easily judged within a few short minutes of conversation. Thriller. Boring contemporary. Paltry mystery. Tabloid.

Dangerous or not, Damien is no different from the egos and corporate giants I decipher for a living.

"How much do you pay them, your models?" I wonder, employing my usual trick of rapid-fire questioning. "Do you sleep with them? Do you photograph them first? How do you get them to look like that—"

"Do you think this is a game?"

Oh. I cross my arms to guard against his tone. So he doesn't want to play. Fair enough. I'll have to take a page from Daddy's book and judge him off his cover alone.

My eyes narrow, seeking out what little detail I can in the dark. I expect to find him brooding—most artists are.

Instead, he's pensive. His voice betrays the impatience his body does not. He's all smooth lines and lean muscle, reminding me of a predator benevolent enough to hiss in warning before pouncing for the kill.

"Not a game," I concede. "As I said, the painting is mine. You can't have it."

"Oh?" That word again. So simple. So subtle. His voice is like music, containing more subtext in the underlying melody than the actual lyrics. "I would ask you to reconsider, Ms. Thorne."

"I'll think about it."

"And perhaps I'll *think* about returning something of yours."

My throat goes dry as I process his tone. Then I remember.

Ice washes over me with an intensity I've never felt in my entire life. Not all those years ago in the forest. Not moments ago when I found an intruder in my home.

For the first time ever…I forgot. Simon. His game.

I forgot.

"W-was there something on my doorstep?" Even I can hear the tremor in my voice.

And like a shark sensing a single drop of blood, he cocks his head. "*Sí.* There was… A bit old for dolls, aren't you?"

No.

As I watch, he withdraws something from his pocket and my heart twinges in recognition: a porcelain doll with carefully coiffed blond hair.

"Sammy," I whisper, horrified. "Give it to me!" I reach for it but stop short, inches away, as his posture shifts.

"Should I?" He's running his fingers through the doll's hair, disrupting her neat coif. Simon always took care to style it the same way. Like she did.

"Give it back." My breaths quicken, shallow and ineffective. The doll's face is visible from here, illuminated by a strip of neon-yellow light. Glassy eyes. Painted grin. Rosy, red cheeks. It's a replica, but one so damn close to the real thing...

"You can have her if you want," Leslie pleaded, grasping at my hands. "Just don't be mad at me."

No! I fight the memory back with bared teeth. "Give it back—"

He lifts the doll by her tiny waist, and I lunge forward. At the last second, he pulls her out of my reach, testing just how much I want it. Enough that a ripping sound echoes as I clench her tiny body in my fist and try to tug her free.

But he's too strong. Without warning, he stands, shrugging me off as easily as a gnat. "Sammy," he murmurs, a chuckle lacing his tone. "It even has a name?"

The color drains from my cheeks. She does. We have a ritual, Simon and I. His favorite tool of torture is my own memory. Samantha. She was Leslie's favorite character to spin our games of house around. Such a perfect doll, ten times more expensive than anything I could ever afford.

Sammy, beautiful Sammy, was the source behind our only fight ever.

Sammy, stupid Sammy, was the reason Leslie died.

"*Please*," I rasp, knowing I could never overpower him. "Give it back."

"I will. When you return what is mine." He turns while manipulating something in his free hand. Slender, thin. Long. It extends as I watch: a white cane he taps against the floor.

"I'll show myself out," he says at the exact moment I utter, "You're blind?"

"Have a wonderful night, Ms. Thorne." He starts for my door, using the cane for guidance.

So the eye covering isn't for dramatic effect. Yet I'm unconvinced he isn't putting on an act. He moves too confidently, every motion smooth and assured. Almost like he learned the layout of my apartment down to the slight right angle one must turn to enter the foyer and approach the still open door.

"Pleasant dreams," he tells me as he crosses the threshold.

It's only when he's gone that I remember how to move. I slam the door in his wake and engage the lock. I'm not afraid. *Liar*, my body claims. Muscle and bone go limp in defiance and I'm forced to brace my weight against my palms to catch my breath.

Tap. Tap. The tap of his cane forms a morbid tune that tracks the departure of Damien.

Eventually, the sound trails off and I'm alone again.

With Simon? It's his time to shine, after all. Day two. Sammy was the second present. Dread solidifies in my stomach; I know where I'll find the third.

I push from the door and sway to regain my balance. It's like I'm transported back all those years ago. Locked in the dark, forced to feel my way through touch. Forward, using the wall as a guide. To the left. Down a little more. Right. The floor beneath me switches to smooth tile, and I feel along the wall for the light switch.

Harsh iridescence plunges everything into stark relief. The white walls I never bothered to paint. The pristine countertops still stained with blood. The broken mirror displaying fractured pieces of a hundred different Julianas.

I had the workers skip this room for a reason.

Simon still hasn't grown tired of this hiding place. My present waits in plain sight, lying across the sink basin. A single rose, snow-white. A red ribbon encircles the stalk, choking it. The allusion is less obvious than Sammy, but it's memorable nonetheless. A white woolen hat kept brown curls warm paired with a long scarf in a bloody shade of red. *Her* red.

I'll humor Simon tonight. I don't run screaming from the room or crawl to my stash of wine. My exhausted body deposits me there, right beside the door, and I sit and stare. I won't remember fully—not yet.

There is still one more puzzle piece to be delivered.

One more day to play the game.

He'll win in the end. He always does.

And in a year, we'll play again.

SIX

*I*t's one of those mornings that pounces, going right for the jugular, ushering in another day of toeing that invisible boundary between hunter and hunted. Simon claims nightfall. It's only fair. I'll have to leave my suite before sundown and return after, just in time to open my final present.

Finding a diversion shouldn't be such a hard task.

I could take Daddy up on his offer and visit more often. Let him see how happy and wonderful I am. He doesn't have to worry, no siree.

Or…

I can crawl on my hands and knees into my bedroom and drink Moscato straight from the bottle. Imbibed with liquid courage, I manage to stand using my bedframe as a crutch and stumble into my closet.

Without bothering to shower, I peel off my stale birthday dress and pull on a black sweater and pants—but I can't shake the feeling that something is missing as I enter the kitchen. While the coffee maker runs, I lean against the counter and tap my foot. Eventually, my fingers join in, abusing the granite like a makeshift piano. I can't put a name to the sensation building in my veins. It's almost like I hear a clock counting down the hours to some unknown event. *Tick. Tock.*

My coffee starts to pour. The steady drip of liquid into the pot feeds the building suspense like a match over a flame.

Drip.

Drop.

A knock on the door echoes to silence as the last few dregs of coffee anticlimactically drip down to join the majority steaming in the pot.

"Who is it?" I call to no response.

Strange. I don't get visitors. Not ones who come announced through the front door without the aid of a shadowy reputation or stealth to hide behind. Damien? I swallow hard and reluctantly leave the caffeine behind.

A glance through the peephole reveals the face of a stranger. Not Simon. Certainly not Damien. This man is younger, with closely cropped brown curls and a wary smile.

"Delivery for Juliana Thorne," he declares, offering up a potted plant when I crack the door.

The flowers, branching from twisted stems, are small and white. More delicate than Simon's symbolic rose, and nothing like the carnations Daddy sends.

"They're beautiful." I start to finger a wayward petal.

"I wouldn't do that if I were you," the courier warns. "This stuff is oleander. Really toxic. Here—" He juggles the plant on one hand and withdraws an envelope from his pocket with the other.

My name is written on it. I accept both and the man disappears before I can voice a single question.

Not that I have to. Flowers and mystique seem to be the calling cards of one artist in particular.

Though I must give the man credit. He knows his floral arrangements. Oleander blends in beautifully with the muted colors of my kitchen. White over gray and poison over granite make a splendid combination. Who knew?

I pour myself a mug of coffee and take my time peeling the envelope open bit by bit. Inside, I find a black card almost entirely covered in painted versions of my deadly, white flowers. Running my fingers over the designs barely convinces me they aren't real, each one lavished with detail. I can still smell the fresh acrylic. Still see the deliberate, careful strokes of the artist lurking within every line and streak of ivory. Inside the card is a simple message written in a stark, uniformed script.

Sammy and I hope you reconsider—D.

Of all the emotions to feel, intrigue shouldn't be one of them. Did the blind man write his own threatening message?

My racing heartbeat distracts me from pondering the answer. It hammers away at my eardrums. *Thump. Thump.* Rough parchment and dried paint brush my fingertips as they continue to stroke the tiny flowers. Despite the courier's warning, I'm afraid the artificial oleander might pack the most potent punch. Its tiny vines and leaves invade my thoughts, planting dangerous ideas. Like the memory of the card in my pocket and the address of a certain artist's gallery. Images of doll-like eyes and porcelain skin. Red. Roses. Death.

And my actual doll he stole.

Simon's time is nearing, but two additional cups of coffee don't ease the transition of time. Minutes linger, and I'm left without a distraction. Alone in an ocean of idleness without a paddle.

Writing. I could try that. But when I finally fish a pen from a kitchen drawer, my first impulse isn't to jot down notes for a new campaign. It's a name. I write it out in black ink, arranging the letters over a napkin. *Damien. Thank you for the flowers,* I start to pen. Halfway through, I stop and toss the makeshift note into the trash.

I return to my bedroom, standing upright this time. The woman I spot in the full-length mirror near my bed looks like a perfect representation of confidence. Cool exterior. Watering, bloodshot eyes...

Shit. I rub them on my sleeve and turn my attention to my extensive wardrobe. Oleander. I can't get the pure color of it out of my head, though I only have one ensemble in the same lethal shade. A dress bought for some unremarkable occasion and promptly shoved to the back of my closet. I extract it out by the hanger and eye it warily. It's a simple sheath dress with a plunging neckline. Far too daring.

Out of morbid curiosity, I try it on, and I'm unsettled by the results. My hair spills across the scalloped top like blood, unseemly against such a blinding shade of white. Surround me with flowers and I could be one of Sampson's paintings.

Dress me in blue and I'd be the perfect doll for Simon.

Seal my eyes shut with glue and I'd be Leslie.

The thought forces me to remember my third present. I find it in the bathroom, lying on a bed of glass shards. I gingerly remove the ribbon and wrap it around my wrist: a glowing reminder. The rose, I tuck behind my ear.

My reflection greets me from the destroyed mirror, but I don't recognize the person I find. Someone stupid enough to visit one monster in her spare time before another comes calling.

I grab my coat from the hall closet and find the business card inside the pocket. A minute-long call is all it takes to have my usual town car service send a driver around. Ten minutes later, I'm stepping out from the shelter of the Lariat and heading across town.

Damien likes his privacy. His haunt is a tall building near the waterfront. Dark brick and sleek glass form an impressive structure that I assume is privately owned when I reach the entrance and find both glass doors locked. There's no sign. Merely an intercom affixed on the outside wall. When I press the button marked *call*, a gruff voice comes from the speaker, laced with static.

"What do you want?"

That's a damn good question.

"Name?"

I jump as the voice comes from the speaker again. Clearing my throat, I answer, "J-Juliana Thorne."

Silence. I'm left standing there with my thumb poised over the silver button while the rest of my body is angled toward the car. I should leave. I will. My hand falls just as an electric buzz comes from the door, followed by the click of a lock disengaging.

"Come in." The speaker crackles. "Take the elevator to the third floor."

With one last glance at the car waiting behind me, I enter the building, fighting a sense of trepidation with every step. It's surprisingly clinical for the lair of a madman. The entrance opens onto a small hallway, which branches off in two directions. One leads to a dead end, while the other stops before a set of silver elevator doors.

I strike the button for the third—and topmost—floor, and seconds later, the doors part, revealing another hallway, this one carpeted in a dark shade of gray and lined with black walls. The only illumination is cast by lit sconces glowing a dim, fiery orange.

How melancholic. Did he decorate with the intention to intimidate in mind?

It's only as my heels sink into the plush flooring that I remember his blindness. *Supposed* blindness. I close my eyes, imagining how this view might "appear" to someone like him. Even behind my eyelids, the muted color scheme makes the darkness feel heavier. Thicker. My skin heats when I near a sconce. I pass it, the world cools again. Hot. Cold. The dueling sensations go to war over my flesh with every step I take. My fingers graze the smooth surface of the wall, only to suddenly meet air. A doorway?

I open my eyes.

Damien likes his workspace dark. Few lights illuminate what the daylight filtering in through sparse windows doesn't. Wooden floors pick up my footsteps and broadcast them loudly to the man at work in the center of the room, hunched over a wooden table.

Behind him, arched windows display swaths of the waterfront and little else. The room itself is massive, with vaulted ceilings that amplify the slightest disturbance. Like my thready breathing and his heavy sigh.

Though he's wearing jeans, there's nothing at all casual conveyed by the ensemble. Tension enhances the muscle revealed by the short sleeves of his gray shirt. Every piece is tailored to perfection, impressive even from this distance.

The man treats his body like his art, no stitch placed without intent.

"You came." He pushes back from the table and inclines his head in my direction. "Though I expected you to contact me by other means. I shall have to remind Carla as to the importance of my privacy."

My heart lurches. Charming Carla. Have I unknowingly gotten her into trouble?

"I insisted," I lie, disguising it behind a forced laugh. *Haha.* "She thought I'd appreciate your art."

"Now that is interesting," Damien muses. He strokes his thumb along his chin. The fingers of that hand are black at the tips. From sketching, judging from the materials spread out before him. He's working on a large piece of paper using only sticks of charcoal placed at strategic positions. "I've never questioned Carla's judgment before."

He's unreadable behind the blindfold, and his neutral tone obscures whether he means the statement as a threat. Left to decipher him blindly, my nerves dance with indecision. To tense or not? Fight or flight?

I settle on neither. For now.

"Anyway," he continues, waving his hand through the air before grabbing a piece of charcoal with it. "All that matters is you've changed your mind. I'll make the arrangements to return my painting and you may have your doll—"

"No. I haven't changed my mind… What are you doing?" I draw closer to him when I shouldn't.

He started sketching again while he spoke, and the rough contours catch my eye. A woman. She's outstretched over white paper, her limbs formed of inky black. Unseeing eyes stare out as her lips contort around a final, gasping breath.

"It's beautiful." The words spill from me without permission, but in my head, they aren't quite a compliment. Beautiful. Ugly. Grotesque. "How can you—"

"Don't touch." He grabs my wrist before I even register reaching out. How? He tugs when I try to snatch the limb away, tightening his grip. "Beautiful," he says tacitly. "I thought you said it was *terrible*."

I twist my wrist to no avail. He's too strong. The pads of his fingers capture sinew and bone beneath them and press just hard enough to sting.

"Let me go—"

"What are you wearing?" He cocks his head as if sensing something that I can't, his nostrils flared.

"Get off!" I tug my arm again. "Let go."

"*Perdóname*. What are you wearing?"

Snark is my first instinct. "A dress," I spit out.

"And?" Impatience seeps from him like the poison from my oleander. Invisible. Deceptive. Like he's hunting for something.

"And…" I look down at my feet. "Heels."

He frowns, still unsatisfied with my answer. "And?"

"And nothing." Then I remember my newest gift. Swallowing hard, I add, "And…a rose in my hair."

He lets me go and his hand drifts toward a piece of charcoal before he flattens it against the table instead. "I take it that you appreciated my gift."

He laughs and the deep, guttural rumble robs me of my senses for a brief moment. I blink. He and the rest of the room disappear. Reappears. Disappears.

With my eyes still closed, I utter my reply. "Very much so."

A sound catches in his throat. *Ah.* Not quite a laugh. He's amused. He's annoyed. "*Por favor.* Tell me, what color is your dress, Juliana?"

"Why?" Trying to decipher him triggers a dull throbbing in my temples.

The discomfort isn't because of the question itself, however. It's how he asked it. Politely. Curiously.

"Black," I finally admit.

Another partial laugh is my reward. "A lie."

I glance at him sharply. "How can you tell?" Maybe he isn't so blind after all.

His gaze isn't on me, but focused straight ahead, toward the light coming in from one of the windows. "I know."

"Well, then you should also know that I've decided to keep the painting." Have I? Only now do I feel like examining my reasons for coming here in the first place. To evade Simon, possibly. To thank Mr. Villa for his thoughtful gift. To hide. To concede. To refuse. "You can burn the doll."

"I'm very sorry to hear that, Ms. Thorne." His tone dips an octave deeper than before. Picking up a thinner stick of charcoal, he continues to sketch, adding detail to an outstretched hand. There goes at least one mystery: He *has* to see. There's no other way he could be so precise. "I trust you can show yourself out."

Squaring my shoulders, I turn to do just that—but I've barely gone a step before he calls out, "By the way, Juliana. You sound different in white."

"How did you..." My footsteps falter, my heart clenching painfully. "Fine," I croak rather than accuse him of lying out loud. "You want your painting back? Let's make a fair trade, then. You give me something I want. I give you what you want."

"Your doll isn't sufficient enough?" he counters.

"It's already served its purpose." I think of Simon and shudder. He couldn't have planned a more memorable way to present his Sammy replica than this—held hostage by a newer monster. "So do you want to trade or not?"

"Trade. Information, perhaps? Like that of your father and his reputable donors and the careful, gilded cage he's built around you that you can't even see?"

"No," I say hoarsely. "Don't you dare talk about him—"

"Then what?" He's still sketching when I turn around, his posture angled toward the drawing, conveying complete disinterest in me. "What could the daughter of Heyworth Thorne want from me?" he wonders.

My answer escapes in a rush. "I...I want you to paint me."

Do I? The veracity of the answering pinch in my stomach surprises me. Yes.

"Paint you?" He sounds too soft. Like I suggested he stick a brush up his ass rather than use one.

I'm flashed back to last night. What was that word he used? Insult.

"If you even can," I add, returning to the table one halting step at a time. "For all I know, it could be a ruse, just like your so-called blindness. Dad—Judge Thorne told me that you really use them to—"

"I'm sure he told you plenty of things about me," he says dismissively. "I could tell more about him."

The implied threat has the effect of shutting me up.

"So the woman who calls my art terrible wants me to paint her. Would this piece hang in your father's office, I wonder? A gift for when he runs again for mayor?"

"How did you know that?" The second I reply, I recognize his statement for the bait it was.

"Only a man as conceited as your father would demand more power rather than reflect on his past misuse of it," he smugly retorts. "And only his daughter would desire what she considers terrible."

I attempt to shrug off the venom in his tone but wind up flinching. His accent can cut like a whip when he wants it to. "There are worse things to be called than that."

"Oh?"

"Yes."

Like perfect.

The drawing he's working on now is anything but. It's goddamn terrible. Beautiful lines. Cruel, honest mortality.

"*Por qué?*" He drops the stick of charcoal and it makes a stray line in the wrong place, marring the woman's detailed torso. Then it rolls off the table and hits the floor, continuing toward me. "And how should I paint you?"

I can imagine the answer he expects: prettily.

"Like them," I say instead—and there is no need to elaborate. I want him to paint me naked. Dead. Honest.

This time, Damien doesn't reply. His fingers fan out in front of him, trapping the sketch beneath them. Then they curl, crumpling the drawing into a ball, which he tosses onto the floor.

"Explain," he says, invoking that harsh, commanding tone.

My lips part, words spilling out on cue. "How do you see them?" I'm closer to the table before I realize it, bending to snatch the discarded sketch. Despite how protective he seems to be of his art, he doesn't warn me away. "How do you pose them?"

Another question goes unanswered as I unfurl the drawing and observe it up close.

"Come here."

My eyes cut to him sharply. *No,* every nerve in my body warns. He's got them on red alert, humming with nervous energy. "W-why?"

He raises his hand and crooks one beckoning finger. "Come."

"No," I say. *Liar.* I'm already inching closer to the opposite end of the table.

A blur of motion is all I register before my chin is in his grip. Startlingly warm fingertips tilt it expertly while five more come to graze the side of my jaw.

I suck in a breath. He has the softest hands I've ever felt. Like velvet. Hands that must wear gloves to perform any menial tasks. Hands that could only commit the most sterile of murders.

Dangerous, sinful hands.

"You want me to paint you?" His breath fans my cheeks, unbearably warm.

"Yes..." For some reason, I don't shy from his touch. I let him examine me. There's more to the manipulation of his fingers than a desire to intimidate. They capture the curve of my face. The swell of my cheek. My hairline.

Finally, he sits back and opens a drawer concealed on his end of the table. From it, he fishes out a fresh sheet of paper, and with the thinnest strip of charcoal, he makes a few soft lines. Gradually, a woman's face takes shape. It's round, her features average. Some might call her attractive if it weren't for her exaggeratedly wide eyes and pursed lips.

Recognition hits in a slow-burning realization. It's me.

Then again, she isn't me.

There's fear in her eyes, more apparent the more of her he reveals in lines of black. She's thin—too thin—standing tall. Her hands are outstretched, grasping at the air in front of her. Unlike his other creations, she's fully dressed in a simple, white sheath dress.

I'm tempted to accuse him of feigning blindness again—but the details are vague enough to be guesses. Besides, it's the woman's expression upon which he lavished the most insulting attention. Her dour, terse frown could only be described as...lost.

Or terrified.

"Is this meant to scare me?" My voice rasps. I find myself licking my lips and swallowing hard to ease a sudden dryness in my throat. I've been standing here, watching him longer than I've realized. The angle of light coming in through the window is sharper, dimmer, and my ankles throb, confined in my heels.

"Scare?" With a sigh, Damien finishes off the last stroke. Then he lifts the drawing and offers it to me.

I scoff. That caricature looks nothing like the woman I strive to be. She's pathetic. Weak. She's the person I want to drown in a bottle of wine. "That's the best you can do?"

As I reach for it, Damien withdraws the page just beyond my range. "Uh-huh." He nods once, indicating my body, I presume. Namely what I'm still clutching in my fist. "Exchange."

I consider tossing both scraps of paper into the trash. I should.

In the end, I let the discarded drawing fall onto the table within his reach, and he lets me pull the fresh drawing from his grip.

"Do you feel that was a fair trade?" he asks, while I retreat toward the light of the nearest window and observe his distorted creation up close. She's not me—despite how uncannily familiar her nose is.

She's not.

"I expended the energy to create both drafts," he continues. "You stole one without permission and yet bartered it for another. So..." From the corner of my eye, his silhouette flickers. "Is this a fair trade?"

Ignoring him, I sweep my gaze along the drawing again. Then I tear it in half and let both pieces fall. "There," I tell him, unnerved by how patiently he's sitting, no emotion revealed whatsoever. "Now they're both unwanted. Besides, I thought artists like a challenge. That looks nothing like me."

"Is that so?" He stands swiftly, catching me off guard. He must have had the cane propped against the table, because it's in his hand now. It extends, tapping the floor before him, and he advances on me far more quickly than he should be able to.

Instinct seizes control of my feet, propelling me backward. Back...back. Until I hit a wall and can't go any farther. I'm forced to watch as he approaches, but I'm offered no warning when he touches me this time. Bold and sure, his fingers graze the side of my throat, tracing the pulse thrumming there.

"I'm not so sure of that..." His mouth tilts downward, his thumb pressing harder.

"W-what are you doing?" I avert my gaze to the opposite wall—but I don't move. For some insane reason, I endure the second appraisal, and this time, he extends his search.

Down my throat, following the midline of my collarbone. A ragged gasp escapes my lips as unfamiliar heat creeps through the satin over my rib cage. Too low. Then even lower, down to my hips. He keeps the contact featherlight. Barely noticeable.

Yet inescapable.

Finally, he steps back, and his cane retracts, able to be slipped inside his pocket.

"I would not question my sight if I were you, Ms. Thorne," he declares, the corner of his mouth quirked. He's amused once again.

"With all due respect, Mr. Villa, I don't feel like arguing sight accuracy with a blind man."

"And you shouldn't," he bites back. "How frustrating it must be to have your sight and yet not be able to see things as they are."

"What's that supposed to mean?"

He laughs and shakes his head. "I do not think you'd understand."

Before I can voice a comeback, he reaches for me. Two quick fingers capture the rose behind my ear and yank it free.

"Stop!" My trembling fingers swipe at nothing.

He's too quick. His free hand crushes the bloom, molesting the petals. In pale clumps, they litter the floor, finally followed by the discarded stem.

"Roses are not your flower," he declares.

"Oh? And oleander is?" The bravery I hope my voice carries falls flat. My gaze won't leave Simon's mutilated flower. My reminder. Coherent thoughts scatter like those broken petals. I'm clenching my fingers, aching to shove the remains together and somehow make it whole again. "I'm leaving—"

"Do you want to know why I paint my subjects nude?" he wonders suddenly.

"Considering that you supposedly 'see' through touch, I can imagine why."

Rich laughter echoes in the wake of my irritation. He deploys the reaction the same way someone else might a narrowed gaze or terse expression: as a warning.

"People hide behind layers," he explains. "The more you remove, the more of the real person is revealed underneath. For instance, the loss of a single rose can strip a woman bare in ways she doesn't realize."

"Is that so?" I cross my arms over my chest. "Frankly, Mr. Villa, this conversation is becoming inappropriate—"

"You want me to paint you," he says over me. "And yet, *frankly*, Ms. Thorne, there is nothing about you worth painting. I capture people. Not their masks, and you have crafted a rather elaborate one if I may say."

"E-excuse me?" No one talks to me like this. I can't remember the last time a man even raised his voice to me other than the recent voicemails. It's a benefit of living in a cage of glass, steel, and concrete. Money creates an imaginary world with padded edges and gossamer chains.

The rules are simple: ignore and pretend.

"I've changed my mind," I say, turning on my heel. "You can have your damn painting *and* the doll. Have a good day, Mr. Villa—"

"Strip." The command comes so softly that I had to have imagined it. A cruel joke played by a twisted mind?

But no.

The air feels heavier and my cheeks are on fire. Wounded pride won't let me move without first choking out a question. "What did you say?"

"I told you to strip," he replies, his voice eerily calm. Almost taunting. "Unless you're afraid of the person you're hiding beneath that priceless designer frock."

"Afraid?" I force my own bit of carefree laughter, but the notes ring hollow. "So you're a sexual deviant as well as a hack—"

"I'll say this once," he interjects. "You can insult me all you want, but never my art."

My spine stiffens at the subtle shift in his tone. A shout wouldn't carry the same level of malice. No. He's honed intimidation into an art form.

"Now, I'd like for you to leave. *Adiós.*"

My heels rock against the floor, but I don't budge. Instead, I watch myself from the window's surface. Proud, perfect Juliana.

He's a liar. If only he weren't a better one than I am.

My fingers sweep along my hip, gathering my skirt between them. I move slowly, registering the cold air with every inch of fabric I wind up my torso. When the material clears my head, I let it fall with a resounding thud. At the same time, my gaze goes to Damien. I want him to blush. Or leer in the chilling revelation that he isn't blind. Anything but sigh.

With the aid of his cane, he returns to the table and sits. He snatches another sheath of paper from the drawer while his free hand beckons sharply. "Come here."

"W-why?" Anxiety surges beneath my skin, whipping my nerves into a frenzy. What the hell am I doing? Standing half-naked before a stranger, for one. Of all the things to consume my attention, it shouldn't be his disinterest.

"I'll ask you one more time to come here." He sounds like he's scolding a naughty child and considering withholding a toy.

"What are you going to do?" Regardless of my unease, I come to the opposite end of the table, and he nods to the expansive surface before him.

"Lie down."

A refusal springs to my lips but dies before I can voice it. Turning my back to him, I perch myself on the edge of the table and shift my weight so that he's on my left. Inch by inch, I lower myself backward until the chilled wood bites into my skin.

"Don't relax," he warns as his hand settles over my outstretched wrist. His fingers give the flesh an examining brush. "I want you to feel."

The request haunts me as my gaze flickers up to the shadowed ceiling. These days, I don't have time to feel. I project—confidence, fearlessness, perfection.

Who am I without that so-called priceless frock crumpled on the floor?

I doubt a blind psychopath can tell me.

"What are you doing?" I croak as his touch continues up my arm, encroaching on my collarbone.

He says nothing. Every now and again, I hear the telltale hiss of charcoal scraping parchment, but I'm not brave enough to check his progress for myself.

Instead, my eyes drift shut as if of their own accord. Darkness and silence are the only tools I have to decipher the events taking place around me. Electricity humming. Artificial heat blasting. Hot, smooth skin exploring my own.

It should feel worse. I can't escape the thought. Having him touch me should feel worse than it does. If only there weren't a discernible method to his madness. He touches me where he must, gleaning what secrets my flesh contains before moving on to another area. Scratch, scratch goes the stick of charcoal, tracking his progress.

My arms. Shoulders. Hands.

My breasts…

"W-wait!" I can't smother a cry when he cups one with his palm. "Don't—"

"Leave, or stay," he warns, his palm stilling.

My heart races, threatening to hammer right out of my chest. Somehow, I manage to lie still, and he continues his study of me. He's not slow and deliberate with this part of my anatomy, however. One pass is all he makes before moving on. You've sketched one set of breasts, I guess you've sketched them all.

It's my hips that consume the most attention.

"You have scars," he says, unable to disguise a note of curiosity. "From what?"

None of your business. The words don't come out, and he continues his groping without waiting for a response.

When his touch finally withdraws, the sounds of sketching pick up in earnest. Bold, sure strokes. Smaller, light dashes.

I let my mind wander, trying to envision what he comes up with. All I can picture is a shapeless mass of shadow. Somehow, I know when he's finished without him having to say a word. My eyes open slowly, and I roll away from him, crossing my arms over my chest.

Pitch-black windows give a vague inkling of how much time has passed. Hours at least.

When I finally look over my shoulder at him, his hands are braced flat against the table and the tips of his fingers are blacker than ever. He touched me like that, tainted with the stain. I'm dotted in more fingerprints than the actual paper —like a canvas.

"Well?" He gestures to the finished drawing, his head cocked as if listening for my reaction, and I'm painfully aware of my rapid, shallow breaths.

I look down, biting my tongue. He made this sketch larger than the last. It consumes nearly the entire page: the result of shading and smeared charcoal.

The woman staring up at me is an enigma. I don't recognize her. Or maybe I don't want to. She's more like a specter: someone I catch only glimpses of before I banish her with red lipstick and my custom wardrobe.

Someone I hide. Scorn. Shun.

But she gets her revenge now. Damien's sought her out and pushed her presence right in my face.

"I request that we end this visit now, Ms. Thorne," he says, rising to his feet. After extending his cane, he heads for the door, steadier than I feel. "Keep the scrap paper, but forget this address. Best regards to your father. I'm sure it will be quite the media spectacle when he announces his return to politics."

He's gone through the doorway before I fully register the intent of his words. *Definitely* a threat that time.

What's more alarming is my reaction. I'm not trembling when I finally place my feet on the floor and pull on my discarded dress.

I fully intend to leave the drawing, and I make it all the way to the elevator doors, wandering a hallway devoid of Damien. My finger strikes the button. The elevator arrives.

But the doors close without me inside.

There's no one there to witness my return to that lone table. Upon retrieving the sketch, I fold it carefully, tucking it against my palm.

Maybe I'll throw it away.

Or maybe I'll keep it for Simon.

No matter how many gifts he's sent and no matter how many years he's haunted me, he's never seen this woman.

SEVEN

$\mathcal{I}$ escape Damien's lair only to reenter a neon jungle that doesn't appear to have missed me any. Or so I think. I'm shocked to find a town car waiting patiently near the curb—the result of an overzealous driver? Or Damien himself? I don't ask, though when I climb into the back seat, the clock on the dashboard proclaims it's after midnight.

Then I remember. Panic racks my spine, though it could be pity. Or terror. Poor Simon. For the first time in twenty years, I've stood him up.

Worse than that: I've forgotten all about him...*again.*

Were I in my right mind, I would urge the driver to rush home, hoping to make amends with my deranged torturer before time ran out.

I'm too tired now. My eyelids flutter, weighed down by hours of tension. I've never felt so worn. So apathetic.

As the driver pulls before the Lariat on cue, I watch it loom above me in all its glory. "Never mind," I hear myself say without reaching for the door. "I think I'll stay at the Harrison tonight."

It's a less prestigious hotel on the other end of the city. One favored by the riff-raff, some might say. A place someone like me would rarely deign to stay at.

And the one place where Simon won't look for me now.

*M*onday is a workday. There's no sheltering from it beneath thin sheets or a worn duvet. Sluggish with dread, I drag myself from my suite at the Harrison and return to my apartment just as dawn kisses the horizon. I round the corner near my suite with my hands already outstretched, prepared to face my punishment.

Only to find my doormat empty.

My throat tightens, constricting what little oxygen I manage to breathe in. It's a bad sign—the first of many. My final present of the year isn't waiting for me on the kitchen counter beside my potted oleander. Neither is it on the glass coffee table in the living room.

Bitter apprehension suffocates the remaining air from my chest as I start toward my bedroom. It's raining out. Icy drops speckle the windows, the view beyond them. The world below becomes a blurred kaleidoscope of motion and noise, like a merry-go-round on warp speed. My apartment, however, is frozen in time, and I can't escape the insane feeling that everything, down to my white carpet, is watching me.

Waiting for something.

The door to my bedroom is cracked, just how I left it. However, the maid came while I was gone. She made my bed and tidied the closet, leaving her trademark card behind. No signs of Simon here.

Not even in the bathroom. Inside it, all I find are broken glass and dried blood.

I flinch as muffled notes of piano music begin to play. "Moonlight Sonata." I follow the melody back into the living room and find my cell phone, clinging to the last cell of battery life. I cringe at the time I find flickering on the screen. Late. So late. My boss is the one calling, but I don't answer.

If I shower now, I can make it to the office in less than twenty minutes. Wishful thinking, as it turns out. It takes more soap than usual to make me feel clean. Naked and dripping with moisture, I attempt my makeup.

First, a blood-red lip, like usual. Poreless foundation. Powder, powder.

Wrong. Lining my eyes with kohl doesn't chase the redness in them away. Beads of liquid seep from behind them, ruining my attempts to create a fearless smoky eye. I try again. Again.

Damn it.

In the end, I settle for washing my face and slicking my hair into a bun. My outfit of choice is a black pantsuit that takes forever to button. I'm still fastening the last one as I hunt for my heels to the soundtrack of my incessant ringtone. Note to self: Lay off the Beethoven. I've never realized how fucking pretentious it sounds before.

Because I'm never late.

The grim thought chases me out onto the street, where I find my town car waiting as expected. However, rush hour traffic foils my timeline. I'm racing into my department forty minutes later to hushed gossip and startled expressions. Someone offers up a nervous hello as I rush into my office, but I don't have the energy to return the greeting.

Focus. I shake my head to clear it and brace my hands over my lap. It's Monday. A new day. One when Simon's game is almost over and I'm free for 363 more until next year rolls around.

Freedom.

The hope plays around my mind as I shuffle from meeting to meeting, working on assignment after assignment. I even stay late, stretching my shift into a twelve-hour day despite how my temples throb and my eyes burn after hours of computer strain. Gradually, the office empties until I'm the only one left behind.

Only now do I slip on my coat and head for the elevators. When I reach the lobby, my lips contort into my trademark smile, ready to wish Gus goodnight. But I round the corner near the main entrance only to find his podium empty, a lady's magazine lying on top. My stomach churns; I've stopped without realizing it. Slowly, I force myself to take a step and shake off the unease racing down my spine. He most likely ran to the bathroom.

Regardless, uncertainty builds with every step I take toward the main doors. Roughly ten feet of space separate me from them. My car is waiting; out front, I spot the ruby glow of taillights. I won't take another detour tonight, to a madman's dwelling or otherwise. I'll go home. I'll be a good girl.

I'll wait my turn. Simon's game isn't over yet.

But this time...I think he sent someone to play with me. Their footsteps are softer, echoing mine. Thwack. Thump. Thwack.

"H-hello?" I call out.

The figure casting the shadow flickering along the wall up ahead is too tall to be Gus. Too slender.

Too fast.

I run, pumping my arms, reaching for the door—but something slams into me before my fingertips graze the glass. I land on my knees, tasting blood, and a split second is all I have to react. *Run!*

There's a side exit directly across from Gus' desk. I lunge for it, but sudden tension on my hair locks me in place as a cry rips from my lips.

"Don't move," someone breathes into my ear, their voice harsh.

And I'm transported twenty years into the past.

EIGHT

We were playing, a code word for competing. Dolls, toys, clothes—the quality mattered more than the game. Mine was a neighbor's hand-me-down, about ten years out of production. I'd done my best to brush out her gnarled, brown hair and arrange her faded, navy dress, but it was no use. Everyone else had the latest plastic creations. Once again, I had to play on the outskirts, designated the "trailer trash" character in this dolly neighborhood.

"Then I'm trailer trash too," Leslie declared, shooting me a smile that displayed her two front teeth. She thought she was coming to my rescue, like always, but therein lay the rub.

No one would ever mistake her designer doll for anything less than one spit out by the finest boutique.

Her doll never dwelled in a house that doubled as a meth lab. Leslie never had to trade her for cigarettes stolen from her parents' stash or spend hours scraping old grime off her with a toothbrush.

"It's late," one of the other girls declared. She began to pack up her toys, signaling to the other girls to do the same.

Once again, I had put my skills as a social leper to good use. As always, Leslie was the only one who stayed behind. She helped me stow my ratty selection of dolls and accessories into my backpack—but like any good friendless pariah, I spurred her attempts to make nice.

"I'm walking home," I told her, preemptively rebuking our customary ride home in her dad's car. "I'm not some stupid, spoiled brat like you!"

Rather than get upset, Leslie simply blinked in that slow, understanding way of hers. Then she gathered up her sparkly bookbag and nodded. "I'll walk too."

The only flaw in my boast was that I had no idea how to walk home. I'd always taken the bus before Leslie's friendship. But even back then, I refused to lose face. So I picked a direction away from the school and started walking while Leslie followed.

We lived close to each other, ironically enough. She was in the brand-new development just outside of town, while I was in the trailer park behind it.

Both areas required a ten-minute trek on a lonely stretch of road that climbed into the hills. What Leslie didn't know was that even my neglectful parents never let me walk home alone. I'd done my best to disguise my unease, marching with my chin jutting into the air.

But bravery couldn't save us from a stranger's predatory intent. We heard him first: heavy footsteps and intermittent whistling. I still remember the tune, the one from the opening of a popular Saturday morning cartoon. It teased us from beyond a border of trees. Louder. Softer.

Until it sounded as though it were being hummed directly into my ear.

And there was no escape.

*P*ain drags me back to the present as something scrapes the flesh of my throat. Something sharp. Thin.

"Don't move," a man growls into my ear between pants. He doesn't sound like Simon—the only shred of comfort I can find. He isn't my monster, and I'm not the same little girl I was twenty years ago. "…want to die…stop—"

Scream! It's the first lesson taught in every self-defense class I've ever taken. Scream. Flail. Fight.

I kick out with my legs and brace my hands against the floor of the lobby, crawling forward, but agony explodes between my shoulder blades, driving the air from my lungs. The stench of body odor betrays just what is pinning me down: my attacker himself.

He's heavy, easily dragging me back. I feel that icy scrape again against my shoulder, biting deeper the more I struggle. A weapon.

Don't look back, a part of me warns. *Run!*

I make myself deadweight, throwing my body against the floor, and his grip loosens enough for me to ram my elbow back, striking something solid. Then I'm stumbling to my feet, racing for the main entrance. I grab a handle and tug, but it doesn't budge. Neither does the other. Shit! They're both locked—only Gus has the key.

Don't panic.

Move.

There!

The side entrance draws my notice again and I lurch toward it, desperate to ignore the shuffling sounds behind me. Air trickles in and out of my lungs as my few options flash across my mind. I'll never outrun him.

So I let myself trip and go down hard. He rushes over, and I roll onto my back. I catch only a glimpse of an unfamiliar face beneath the shadow of a black hoodie. He's tall. Young.

He doesn't even see the kick coming, aimed squarely between his legs. Groaning, he doubles over, and I lunge to the door. It opens, depositing me into a narrow alley beside the office. Blindly, I race past an overflowing dumpster in a frantic race to the street. A lack of noise warns that there's no one behind me.

Yet.

Surging traffic and the distant howling of sirens disguise most sounds, however. I won't hear him until it's too late. Lost in this sea of people, no one would ever notice me scream if he does catch up. They push past me, specters locked into their eternal routines, oblivious to me.

My shoulder throbs. My bottom lip is on fire, bitten in the scuffle. A limping gait carries me to the main street, but I keep going, right past the idling car. The driver is a shadow perched behind the steering wheel, waiting. Watching.

He could be Simon.

Hell, the man marching toward me carrying a briefcase could be Simon. Or the driver honking as he speeds by. Even the figure shoving me aside with an impatient shrug of his shoulder.

He's everywhere.

Air seeps from my lungs, impossible to contain, but somehow, I keep walking. Staggering. Running.

I've never learned my lesson after all these years: I can't escape him. The shadows converge on me as strangers stare. Their attention burns like spotlights, illuminating my path no matter where I go. How fast I run.

To where exactly? I don't know. Not until I'm pounding on a set of glass doors while my hand paws at the silver button of an intercom. A voice laced with static says something from the speaker. Demands something. I should reply. Be collected. Be polite.

But I can't seem to stop banging my fist on the door. A substance paints the glass with every blow. It's dark, appearing almost purple until a passing car's headlights ignite the color, revealing what it is: a bright-red liquid.

Bzzz! The door jolts against my palm, suddenly unlocked. No explanation comes from the speaker, and I don't wait for one. I'm in the elevator before I know it, tracking something over the floor that glints like a morbid breadcrumb trail. The doors close, locking me inside, but I just stare at the buttons, unsure of which one to pick.

Tick. Tock.

Simon's still watching. I can even hear him now, humming into my ear. *Dada, da dum...*

Ding! The elevator rises without me having struck a button. On the second floor, the doors open, revealing a trio of strange men who start inside before they notice me there. Shock alights their stern expressions, and one of them reaches for his breast pocket, his eyes narrowed.

"What in the hell?"

I lunge through the space between them and find myself in another hallway resembling the one above. This one branches into several rooms. The first I pass is narrow, darkened, empty. Light spills from another doorway up ahead. Voices drift out. Deep. Masculine. Accented.

"I've warned you," a man says, his voice chillingly familiar. "Stay out of it. Understood?"

"Why?" Someone scoffs. "Don't you trust me?"

"I don't," the first man replies. "You're sloppy, Mateo, and I'd rather not see you in prison. Have patience. I will handle this."

"You say that as though I enjoy having to beg you for help on my goddamn hands and knees. But you promised me retribution for Mathias. Remember him? Our brother—"

"Stop." The warning isn't directed at me though I freeze paces from the doorway. "It seems as though Julio needs more training."

Damien stands in the center of a room decorated in muted shades. Black leather armchairs form a circle around an industrial-gray coffee table. Steel-gray walls and wooden floors feed the shadows gathered in the corners. Only the light cast from a hanging fixture combats the darkness.

But even it is no match for Damien. The blindfold reduces his expression to nothing more than a stern frown. Emotions seep from him regardless, painting the air like canvas. Alarm. Anger. Confusion?

"Juliana Thorne," he says coldly. "What a surprise. I'm afraid we'll have to cut this discussion short, Mateo." He inclines his head to a man I only notice now.

Tall like he is, but with a thinner face and shorter hair. He eyes me coldly, his upper lip drawing back from his teeth.

"*Gracías*, brother," he snarls. "I can see that you've *handled* this, all right."

"Leave." Damien's tone may be level, but only a fool would challenge it.

His companion draws himself to his full height, squaring his shoulders. On his way out, he slams into me. Hard. I stagger against the wall and slide to the floor. The room blurs, becoming muted colors and harsh shadow. It's a nightmarish painting dominated by one unmoving figure.

"Breathe!" he growls, his voice cutting deep.

I am, aren't I? I can't *stop* breathing. Gasping down air. Choking it back out. Faster. Faster.

Thwack! Stinging pain flares through my cheek and I flinch in shock as frayed nerves reset and register the sudden nearness of an imposing figure.

"I apologize." He slowly withdraws his hand, his frown stern.

It's almost funny how I feel his slap more than anything else. My fingers race to the throbbing skin, tracing the abuse.

"I don't typically humor unannounced visitors." An unsettling mixture of politeness and malice color Damien's tone as expertly as the charcoal he shades his drawings with. "So what brings you here tonight, Juliana Thorne—"

"My birthday's over." The words fall flat. Broken. Then I'm laughing, forced to draw my knees to my chest as the sound racks me to my core.

He says nothing when I finally trail off, waiting. Expectant.

"It's over. It should be over," I blurt out in a rush. "But twenty years. Twenty years. I never missed a night before. Not one."

"What should be over?"

I flinch. The sharp note of curiosity in his tone shouldn't be there—and he's too hard to read without a gaze to search. I'm the one rendered blind against him.

"Nothing," I croak. Just a shadow. Just a nightmare. Just... "My birthday."

If he's confused by the conflicting statements, I can't tell. And his silence only makes it worse.

"I...fell. At work," I add. "The door was locked. It wasn't supposed to be locked. I fell and..." I'm rambling.

He permits it, aptly listening to every word. Pretending to, anyway. No one ever listens. My therapist just reflects to me what I should feel. Daddy only ever hears what he wants. The world demands pretty, shiny words and adjectives to describe whatever petty bullshit they hope to sell. Darkness isn't appealing. It can't be wrapped with a bow and sold with a smile.

So I lied.

Until now.

NINE

Words spill from me like blood—ironic since I'm still bleeding. My shoulder throbs. Salt and copper itch my nostrils, but every truth ripped from my soul stings ten times worse. Maybe because none of it makes any damn sense. I've been playing the world's oldest game of Simon Says for so long, I don't even know where to begin.

Eight-year-old Juliana did her best when rambling to the first responding officer. *"He made us play…"*

I'm less coherent now.

"Three days," I croak. "I just have to play along for three days."

I'm still laughing. Louder. Harsher. Tears mix in, thickening my voice. My chest heaves, but in this moment, I can't smother my cries behind my trembling fingers or in the sleeves of my coat.

I'm sobbing.

And Damien observes it all in his own callous way.

"Don't move."

I jump when he takes a step, but I'm not his target. Without the aid of his cane, he enters the hall, but I remain hunched on the floor, watching the unfamiliar room from behind the border of my knees.

Little decoration obscures its intended use. There isn't even a television or a stereo system. Just black leather furniture and a cold air of business that lingers long after any other inhabitant has left.

One fact is obvious: I interrupted something. How rude of me—but how strange of *him* to let it happen. There were times when even Daddy would send me away while he had company. The mayor's time was expensive after all, what with campaign contributions to schmooze and donors to win over. He'd visit me in the morning, of course, usually with some small token of affection and a reminder to smile!

He would certainly never lower a crystal flute of wine before my nose and urge me to drink.

"Small sips," Damien warns. "This is a vintage Romanée-Conti. Some consider it...overwhelming."

"Th-thank you." My cheeks heat as I accept the glass. The wine swirling inside might as well be liquid gold; I recognize the brand, a bottle of which sells for around thirty thousand dollars—and that's for a recent run. Ironically, I taste nothing as I drain the glass in one sip.

If he's irritated by the disobedience, he hides it well as I set the glass aside.

"Why are you here?"

"I…" I breathe in deeply and exhale. "I don't know."

I should've called Daddy. Or gone home and waited for another morbid reminder from Simon. Instead, I crawled to the lair of an artist whose soft hands disguise more than they should.

I ran to a madman. He stands tall, shrouded by shadow and light, holding his own glass of wine, which he has yet to sip from. Instead, he sets the glass on the coffee table with no difficulty. He must have the layout memorized.

"You're bleeding." His nostrils flare, his frown more pronounced.

"Oh…" I clutch at my arm. "It's a scratch. I-I fell." The lie rings hollow as I finally look at my shoulder.

A long gash slices through the fabric of my designer coat, revealing my torn blouse underneath and a swath of red. The bastard had a knife, I assume as tears flood my eyes. Simon's favorite toy. At least the wound doesn't feel too deep.

"Here."

I blink and find a white strip of fabric dangling from an outstretched hand. Woodenly, I press it against the worst of the bleeding.

"I'm fine," I lie again. The wine has put everything back into perspective, and a new fear blossoms in the spaces of my psyche Simon doesn't infect. It's too close in here. Too quiet with just me and him. I brace my free hand against the floor and start to stand.

"Since you are here, we might as well discuss your previous proposal, Ms. Thorne," Damien announces while I use the wall as an anchor to climb to my feet.

"My...what?"

"Painting you," he says as though art is the most natural topic in the world to move on to after blood. "We can discuss my methods and decide whether or not you agree to my terms. How does dinner sound?"

"You're serious?" My eyebrows rise, my voice still hoarse.

It would help if he laughed. Something to prove he was taunting me outright. Anything other than his cool, unreadable persona.

"Yes," he says. "Dinner. Somewhere public."

"Dinner." I'm a parrot, echoing him in a detached monotone. "Now?"

"Of course." Unperturbed, he nods. "Unless you've changed your mind."

Pain in my fingertips makes me glance down. I've been subconsciously wringing them together, scraping my nails against sore, raw flesh. "I...I don't... I'm a mess."

"There's a bathroom down the hall," he interjects. "First door to the left."

I should scoff at the callous suggestion. Instead, I move on autopilot, following his instructions until I find myself locked inside a surprisingly spacious bathroom. The color scheme leaves little to be desired: dark tile flooring and more gray walls. His choice? Or perhaps the result of a lazy interior designer taking advantage of a blind client. Even before the thought finishes forming, I doubt it's true. Damien is a man few could manipulate.

So the decoration is his choice, then. Perhaps he likes his guests to feel a sample of what he might. A disorienting lack of color. Dizzying monochrome. Little definition to speak of.

It requires me to close my eyes and *feel* to discern anything at all from the stark surroundings. Sleek fixtures and smooth surfaces. Harsh, violent water pressure that easily rinses the blood from my hands. Dim lighting allows me to look at myself in the mirror and not cringe at what I see. If I squint, I can almost find my old self looking back. Perfect Juliana. Forgiving shadows obscure what brighter light wouldn't.

My breathing hitches as the taste of copper burns my tongue. The flesh of my throat aches with the memory of roughly ground fingers from an unknown assailant and the knife he placed there.

I *feel*, and there isn't enough wine within reach to make it all better.

If Mr. Villa has a reservation to uphold, then I make him blow it. I linger, desperately trying to rebuild my shattered façade. Each time, I fail. Try again. Fail harder. Tears mix with cold sweat, coating my cheeks until I can't discern one from the other.

With a sigh, I give up and slip into the hall.

"Ms. Thorne?" He's still waiting for me in that small sitting room and inclines his head as I approach. "Change your mind?"

I finger the sleeves of my coat, sensing the heat his body throws off even from across the room. "It's late. Most places are closed by now anyway."

He shrugs. "It's of no concern. I have a special agreement with the management of this particular establishment. Shall we?"

I can't ignore the expertly concealed dare.

Are you brave enough, Juliana?

I'm not. Ignoring his hand, I step toward the door and clear my throat. "I should go."

"By all means." What sounds polite on the surface holds more depth than his art and I'm instantly on edge. A deaf man could discern the sarcasm in his voice.

I nearly laugh out loud. How could I be so stupid? "And let me guess, the paparazzi are already waiting outside, courtesy of an anonymous tip? Or are they waiting at this so-called restaurant?"

"I assure all of my guests complete discretion and privacy." The statement could be interpreted in so many ways. Some harmless. Others not so much.

"Oh really?"

"You're more than welcome to see for yourself." He's behind me now, his breath on my neck, his footsteps soft against the hard floor. Damn near imperceptible. "Shall we?"

He pushes past me with enviable grace and extends his cane before him. His arm is slightly cocked, perfect for slipping a hand through should I give a damn about propriety.

Spurring the gesture, I follow him to the elevators and through the opening doors. Locked inside with him, I hold my breath until we reach the first floor. He must have called a car when I was in the bathroom, because there is one waiting for us, idling alongside the curb.

I don't know what I expect as we exit the building. Should I grab the door for him? My hand flutters toward the handle, but it's already in his grip. I see that someone wiped away my blood at least.

"After you, Ms. Thorne." He steps back, letting me pass. Then he proceeds to lead the way to the car.

As we approach, the driver circles around to open the door to the back seat. I wait until the man beside me enters first and retracts his cane. It's not too late to run and thumb my nose up at his offer. My body aches. I'm still bleeding.

I'm still terrified.

And he knows it. He leaves little space on the seat for me to claim, confident I'll bolt. When I finally lower myself beside him, I can't deny a sick satisfaction at the confused quirking of his jaw, but his heat creeping through my clothing quickly smothers the triumph.

"May I?" His palm extends toward me, facing upright. "Your arm," he clarifies when I flinch.

My lips part, but in the end, I say nothing and shove his bloodied handkerchief into his hand. He touches my wrist, ghosting higher toward my shoulder. He doesn't discover the wound right away, and he gently probes the flesh beneath his thumb until a hiss escapes my lips.

"You fell?" He sounds skeptical, but I grit my teeth against a retort. "Your coat, *por favor*," he prompts, his voice tighter than I've heard it yet.

My first impulse is to resist as he peels my jacket back—but I am the idiot who got into the car with him in the first place, and I can't be seen in public bleeding and broken.

My fingers shake as I tug at my collar, but he assists me, revealing the thin blouse I didn't intend to be seen in when I threw it on this morning. Knowing he's blind doesn't ease my nerves one damn bit.

It's too close in here. I'm painfully aware of every brush of his unnervingly soft fingertips grazing the rent edges of my blouse.

"Take your arm out of the sleeve."

I turn to the window, disguising how my cheeks flush. At least he sounds more efficient than predatory.

"Fine." I bite my lip and undo the first four buttons, providing enough slack for him to slide the damaged sleeve down my shoulder.

"It isn't deep," he says. How he can tell as much from touch alone? I don't bother asking. "You shouldn't need sutures. Though…"

I wince as he runs his finger directly over the wound, heedless of the blood that coats it.

"This was made with a knife. You were assaulted."

Hearing him say it makes it all too damn real.

"I'm fine." I shrug him off and attempt to snatch the handkerchief back, but he pulls it out of my reach.

"I'm sure you are aware that your father has plenty of enemies. I should take you home. Or at least call the police—"

"Or you can let me out right here and leave me alone."

He pauses as if mulling it over. But the doors remain locked —I'm sure I heard the driver engage them. Tension fills the air, feeding off the inescapable fact that he holds all the control.

"I've humored your valiant attempts to appear unaffected, Ms. Thorne," he says, proving as much. "Don't assume that you can lie to me. Even without my sight, I know that you're trembling. That you came to me so hysterical my doorman broke protocol to let you in."

Hysterical? I grit my teeth. "I'm fine—"

"I know that you were sobbing," he continues over me. "And I played your game by not mentioning it before, but I know you're crying even now."

Damn him. I impulsively swipe at my eyes. They're burning. Wet. Because I'm tired. I barely slept last night. The long work hours have strained my vision and triggered a pulsing headache. That's why.

"You said you *fell*." He voices the statement with a sudden concern that chafes against my already sore pride. "And yet you didn't call your father or the police—"

"I didn't come here for the third degree," I snap.

"*Sí*. So why did you come, then?"

I glare out the window in lieu of answering right away. Blurred buildings pass by in a blend of color. We're somewhere uptown, I assume, hopefully near enough to the Lariat that I could walk to it. My fingers twitch toward the door handle, but something keeps me from grabbing it.

Making a scene now would be both cathartic and utterly stupid.

Not that he'd allow you to embarrass him. The thought comes from someplace deep, impossible to suppress. When I finally let my hand fall, it isn't out of fear. It isn't.

"Are you going to paint me or not?" I demand, changing the subject when the silence becomes unbearable. "I can pay you, of course."

"I don't do it for money." His voice dips down to that unsettling octave. Once again, he's defensive. "And, as I said, we'll discuss my terms and you can decide whether or not you will agree to them. Shall we?"

Huh? Startled, I glance out the window behind him. We've stopped. A high-rise towers above, formed of silver accents and polished glass. The restaurant he mentioned must be inside it. I start for the door, desperate to escape the tension —only to remember that my blouse is undone and I'm wearing one sleeve of my coat. I scramble to assemble myself while Damien patiently waits.

"Take your time, Ms. Thorne," he says, his head cocked, his ears bared to catch my rapid breathing.

He and the driver must have a routine worked out. The other man exits the vehicle first but comes to my end. As I rush out, I turn and find Damien using his cane to maneuver around the car. A part of me wants him to trip. Stumble. Anything to prove that he's human and not infallible.

As if to spite me, he mounts the curb without a hitch.

"Shall we, Ms. Thorne?" He starts for the building's entrance, utilizing his cane. Near the doors, he pauses. "After you…"

I stalk inside with my head held high, expecting one of the quaint, expensive haunts Daddy would drag me to. Places with gilded wallpapers and employees who bend over backward in the hopes of earning a tip to supplement an income that doesn't come close to the cost of a chef's special.

Instead, I find subdued colors and a hushed silence that instantly mutes the noise from the street. The lobby is sparsely decorated but in a way that leaves no doubt in one's mind as to the caliber of humans who frequent this establishment.

Filthy, decadently rich.

"This way." Damien heads forward, using his cane to test the path before him.

A beaming woman in black silk stands behind a silver podium and automatically recognizes my host. "Mr. Villa," she says warmly. "A private room for two, as requested."

It strikes me that the decor looks as though it were ripped right from his studio. Dark walls and polished wood floors illuminated by dim lighting designed to make any visitor feel more disoriented than...

Well, than a blind man.

TEN

A man could bring his enemy here. Or his lover.

It's too intimate. Dark walls form an elegant, if claustrophobic, prison. In lieu of a table and chairs, a leather chaise dominates one wall placed behind a low table —making for a vastly different layout from any restaurant I've frequented.

The only decoration is a row of black curtains shielding one half of the room. All in all, I'm reminded of a private box in a theater and my mind hums with terrifying possibilities. Few things could entertain a man like Damien—and every potential scenario sets my already frayed nerves on fire.

"My usual wine," he requests of the server before seating himself at one end of the chaise. "Anything for my guest?"

I bite my lip to keep from asking for the same. "Water," I choke out. There. Now to keep up the air of being unaffected.

A cursory glance of the room reveals few places to sit without being near him. A spot at the far end of the couch offers the most distance.

"So, you can guarantee the discretion of this place?" I take pains to sound skeptical while gauging his reaction. Damn. Not even a wince. "Unless this was your plan all along? Manipulate me into ruining my father's career?" It sounds so damn obvious when said out loud. "Have a nice night, Mr. Villa—"

"I promised you discretion, did I not?" His face is as stoic as ever, but his hands are clenched at his sides. Once again, I've insulted him. "You can leave," he adds coldly, jerking his chin toward the door. "Or you can join me. The show is about to begin."

Show?

As if on cue, the black curtains part to reveal a sheet of glass behind them: a window.

Confused, I lower myself onto the couch. I assumed the word choice was a taunt, but now? "What is this?"

The main event, apparently. This room overlooks a larger area presumably meant to serve as a stage. Rather than an audience or gallery, rows of mirrors reflect the scene unfolding a good ten feet down below.

"We can't be seen," Damien informs me. "And trust me when I say that no one here gives a damn about your father."

I can guess why. Fixated on the view, I moisten my lips with my tongue and try to steady my breathing. It's rapid and shallow. Am I disgusted? Maybe.

Down below unfolds a scene my father would never expose me to.

Strapped to a black pole is a woman wearing only a leather collar around her neck and nothing else. Her breasts are bared, her body taut with anticipation as a man paces before her, barefoot over black flooring. He's naked as well, sporting a long, black strip of material in one hand. It lashes at the air with every step he takes. A whip.

"What in the hell?" I scramble to my feet, unable to tear my gaze away. There's something primal about the scene. Naked flesh and taut muscle moving fluidly with nothing to disguise it. No protection. No masks. "What is this?"

"Expression," Damien says calmly. "If you are offended, I can arrange for you to be safely returned home—"

"So this is where you get your inspiration from?" I make that word as nasty as I can, oddly satisfied when his jaw clenches. I've broken through that collected exterior. But I have enough sense to regret it as he inclines his head in my direction.

"Not everything is pretty colors to appease your vanity, Ms. Thorne."

"Oh?" I swallow hard and fight to make my voice as haughty and bitchy as I possibly can. "I guess that's how every sick freak tries to justify it—"

"Never call me that." He doesn't have to specify what. *Freak.*

I take another step away from him, toward the door. "Then what should I call you?"

"I suggest you ask yourself the same question. You're offended. Why?"

I scoff. "Because this is disgusting!"

"Why?"

"B-because..." I break off, sensing the trap before he can spring it.

Clever bastard. Once again, he's trying to manipulate me into saying the one thing he seems eager to hear: There's no way in hell I could ever understand him or his fucking art.

"You told me to enjoy the show? But how can you?" I make a show of glancing around the room only to realize that the display is more for my benefit than his. Still, it proves my point. "There isn't exactly a play-by-play."

"Ah." He sits back, suddenly at ease. His fingers form a steeple beneath his chin. "I brought you here for a reason, Ms. Thorne. Put your unique appreciation for the unusual to good use. Narrate." He clips the word between his teeth, an unmistakable dare. A terrifying threat.

"You're disgusting."

He shrugs in a gallant display of indifference. "And you see less than I do. We can agree on those assessments of each other, at least." *And I have you pegged.* The insult stings without him having to voice it aloud. *Spoiled little rich girl.* I could never understand such a twisted, edgy artist.

"They're fucking," I snarl, starting for the exit. "Even blind, you shouldn't need that explained to you—"

"That's not what I asked." His voice cuts the air, harsher than the whip lashing the naked woman, stopping me in my tracks. "I told you to describe it. What you see, as you see it."

"Like how?" I look over my shoulder and feel my cheeks flame. "Naked man. Mounting naked woman. Using his penis to—"

"No." He strikes the leather seat with the flat of his hand. Hard.

I jolt to attention, hating the gasp that trickles from my lips.

"Don't tell me what they're doing. Tell me what you *see*."

"I see…" My gaze returns to the glass. The woman's face is upturned, her eyes wide and unfocused. My heart surges, picking up on her alarm. "She…she's afraid." Before my mind can even travel down a dark road, something in her parted lips catches my attention.

"Why?" Damien wonders, almost as if sensing the same thing I do.

"Because…this is stupid." I turn away, only to be faced with a monster, hunched forward, demanding an answer. His unforgiving snarl offers no escape.

"Why?"

"Stop." I clench my jaw. "I'm not doing this."

"If you lack the ability to articulate a simple, physical act, Ms. Thorne, then by all means. Leave."

And go where?

I was almost murdered tonight. The fact sinks in only now, while two people screw behind me and a madman orders me to play his twisted game of show and tell. I could have died, and no one would be the wiser. Not Daddy. Not the police. Just silence and Simon.

"You have no idea what I've been through."

"Then tell me."

I hate how his voice softens, still cold but less harsh. He's harder to rebuff like this. Harder to ignore.

"Tell you what? How I *feel?*" I spit his word out like it's the naughtiest of expletives. "Right now, I feel like a tool. I *feel* like I'm an idiot for humoring you for this long to be honest."

He says nothing. Waiting. Expecting. He knows I'll run.

Two deliberate steps carry me away from the window as I intend to do just that. Freedom is within reach. So I can't explain why I turn back to the couple again.

The man took the woman off the pole. He has her on her hands and knees, facing our direction. His hand rises and lowers in sharp succession, bringing the whip across her lower back. Something in my stomach twists, like a knot tightening with every blow.

"She's in pain." The voice doesn't sound like me. Broken and monotone; the drone of a sleepwalker in the midst of a nightmare. "But…"

"But what does she feel?" Damien is impatient in his prompting this time.

"She…likes it." I hate the assessment even as it leaves my mouth. "Her mouth is open," I find myself saying, almost to justify the reaction to myself. "She winces when struck, but she's licking her lips. She's not pulling away from him."

If anything, her hips arch into every blow. When the man pauses his assault to swipe a hand through her hair, she shivers into the contact.

"She enjoys it, but she's still afraid."

"Why?" Every quietly uttered question reminds me that I'm not alone. He's there, listening, sensing.

"Because she likes it too much." The man starts to strike her again. With every lash, her entire body quakes, and her teeth capture her lower lip. I recognize the look, admittedly in a different context. "She can't move away. Even if she wants to."

"Oh?" His voice is even softer. "And how can you tell that?"

How? The same way I can look at his paintings and know that, despite the rumors, they aren't part of some money-making scheme.

"Because it's written on her face."

A rush of cool air alludes to the door opening and a woman walks in, balancing a bottle of wine on a tray and two glasses. Without batting an eyelash, she sets the tray down on the table before the couch and pours from a bottle that I assume is twice as expensive as whatever he served me earlier.

When she leaves, I don't wait for Damien's say so to snatch one of the glasses for myself, and then I return to the window, bracing my free palm flat against the glass. My outstretched fingers form a frame, the man and woman trapped between them. Tiny puppets enacting a sick fantasy for the other people no doubt watching them from other private rooms.

"Do you bring all of your subjects here?" I ask the man behind me.

"No." The word lands harshly. "I seek different things from different people."

"And what do you seek from me?"

I already know the answer. Nothing. He merely wants me to stop pretending that I could ever see anything in his art beyond the surface. I'm a superficial bitch—how dare I believe otherwise.

"Tell me what you see," he commands rather than answer my question. "Describe it."

"He's kissing her."

I never stopped watching them. There's no rhyme or reason to their act. No rehearsed movements or enticing grins given to their audience. It's just them, locked in a room, forced to confront their darkest desires.

"He doesn't want to," I add as the man rams his tongue between the blond's lips. "He wants more, but he's holding back for her. To reassure her."

"Of what?" Damien wonders.

"That…" I shy away from voicing more. This is wrong. My eyes dart to the door, but in the process, I catch sight of the man on the couch, his posture rigid, his attention focused solely on me. Reluctantly, I mutter, "That he'll only ever give her what she wants."

"And what does she want?" His question lands more ominously than it should. I'm his pawn being maneuvered like a piece on a gameboard. Checkmate. He seeks surrender.

As for the woman? She wants…

"Freedom," I whisper.

She is on her back now, being herded against the pole, which provides enough stability for her to climb to her feet. The man watches, his whip at the ready. Without warning, he lashes out, striking her across the hips. She leans into the wicked caress, her eyes fixated on her partner, swollen. Begging.

My breath fogs the glass the longer I watch. In all honesty, I've never witnessed something like this before. Sex in its rawest, truest form. No lights. No cameras. Just lust and inhibition.

And Damien.

"My terms," he says as the couple finally collapses against each other, panting and spent. The curtains draw together, obscuring our view until I'm faced with pure darkness. "I require discretion."

"Of course." I grit my teeth, feeling my lips contort into a sneer. "Because the first thing I want to do is tell my father that I'm consorting with you. He warned me that you're a liar," I add, merely to twist the knife. "And a criminal."

And dangerous.

"Our sessions will consist of one per week for a month, an hour each," he continues without missing a beat. "I prefer to meet at night in my studio." He pauses as if to gauge how well I'm following the rapid-fire requests. When I say nothing, he continues. "I also require that my subjects abide by my request during that time."

"And what request would that be?" I face him, curious despite myself. Could this request hold the secret behind his model's morbid poses?

"You submit to me during the allotted time. Fully. I do what I want with you and you do not question."

I can't even pretend that I'm not curious. "In what way?"

He shrugs. "You will be paralyzed during our sessions. A simple drug related to succinylcholine but modified for recreational use. This synthetic version allows you to feel, breathe, and maintain your consciousness, but you will not be able to move."

I'm not familiar with the drug, but I recognize a dangerous scenario when I hear it. This one has all the makings of some sick joke, but he isn't laughing.

"I'll be like this for an hour?"

A slight tilt to his mouth makes heat flood my stomach. "Give or take. It doesn't last long in the body."

"And people actually agree to this?"

"I would understand if you declined." *As you should.* For the first time, I can clearly sense what he doesn't say out loud. *Refuse. Admit it: You can't handle this.*

Of course I can't. But my lips won't move to voice that out loud. I find myself picking imaginary lint off my jacket. "And you say that your subjects let you do anything. Like what?"

His jaw tightens in a way that can only be described as challenging. "Anything I deem necessary."

"Touching?"

"*Sí.*" He leans back against the chaise. "I would need to 'see' my subject."

"How well would you need to see them?" The skin on my neck prickles at the thought. I'm suddenly aware of just how thin this blouse is. Paper fucking thin.

"Thoroughly."

My face is hot. I should take comfort in the fact that he can't see—but I don't. He's aware of each breath escaping my lungs, quickening with every insinuation. A smart woman would be polite. Play coy and avoid mentioning the one subject he seems impatient for me to broach.

"Sex," I say, jumping in headfirst. "Do you sleep with your subjects?"

"Some of them."

"Oh?" I shuffle my heels against the floor in a futile effort to regain my balance. "While they're paralyzed?" I'm picturing it before I can stop myself. Perhaps that's how he gets his sick fix: incapacitating his partners in some twisted bid for control.

But he laughs. "I heed my partner's preference, Ms. Thorne."

"Well, I'm not sleeping with you."

"I wouldn't expect you to." He laughs again, deeper than before. Not to reassure me, but to warn. Sex with me is the last thing on his mind. "Think of it as a research method, one only employed when necessary. I try to give my subjects whatever they need to draw out the emotions I seek."

It's a nice way of putting his perversion—I have to give him that. "And what do you 'seek' from me?"

"Nothing." He shrugs. "Frankly, my painting you would only be to relieve your curiosity. Nothing more."

"Oh?" This time, I recognize the bait for what it is, though it doesn't ease the sting of his trap.

"There's nothing about you that I feel is worth uncovering."

Bingo. I do my best to grit my teeth and let the insult fly by. A normal woman might respond by tossing wine in the bastard's face and catching a car home. I'm low on the wine part. Retaliation is my sole motivation for stalking to the table and refilling my glass.

Before I can aim any of the liquid at him, I take a sip. Then another. "Is that so?" I rasp once half the glass is gone. "Try me."

"You live alone."

"Clever. As if you couldn't tell that much when you broke into my apartment."

"You enjoy living alone. At the same time, you hate it." He pauses pointedly as if to say, *Am I right?*

He's not. But I take another sip rather than humor him with a response.

"You're not comfortable with sex. I'll go so far as to presume that you don't date often, certainly not recently. I'd assume you were a virgin, but most women with your upbringing feel the need to rebel at least once or twice sexually."

Bastard.

"Ah, I guess you employ this party trick with all your guests?" I snap in between sips of wine. Sip. Sip. Sip. My hand shakes, sloshing some down the front of my blouse, but I can't even muster up the energy to curse. He's doing that thing again, talking to me in a way that no one else would dare.

"Your color of preference is black," he continues.

"Strange assumption for a blind man to make." I'm cringing at my rudeness. Whatever. The smug set to his jaw only reinforces my determination to hold my own. He's asking for it. "Unless this is really an act you put on—"

"Black is neutral," Damien says over me. "Imposing. People who wear black are less prone to being approached. Few people will inquire about a black dress versus one in a bright, intriguing shade of pink. In short, it's safe."

His tone implies just what he thinks of that: pathetic.

"So, I guess that makes you an expert on fashion?" I chase the question with another deep sip. My skin still feels hot. Odd. Wine never affects me like this. "What color am I wearing now then, Mr. Villa?"

He cocks his head as if listening for the answer. "Mostly black," he says. "A hint of white."

I cross my arms over my chest. Fucking liar. "So you *aren't* blind—"

"As I said: It's easy to tell when most people wear black," he reiterates. "Think of it as a certain...way of walking. Of talking."

"And the white?" I croak, fingering the collar of my blouse. It's funny. I don't even remember owning it, but sure enough, I found it in my closet, a shade purer than my dress. "I thought you said black was my only color?"

"Preference," he corrects. "And my guess is that...you were distracted."

"Distracted?" The memories of this morning are a blur, minus one inescapable truth. I was thinking of Simon. "What else?" I demand, taking a step toward him and the final sip of my wine. "Tell me, oh wise Mr. Villa."

"You're sheltered. Your father goes to great lengths to ensure that." He laughs darkly, in a way that implies far too much familiarity with that subject. "I wonder if you even know half of the extent."

"Sheltered." The glass slips from my grip. *Ping!* A million shards of glass crunch underfoot. A bit like my pride. "You don't know a damn thing about me."

"Oh?" he murmurs, turning my own haughty phrase against me. "You're sheltered but not innocent. You've suffered," he adds before I can prove him wrong. "And yet you believe that pain gives you license to keep suffering."

"Screw you!" My hand flies out, gathering speed, and the palm strikes his cheek. *Thwack!* I stagger back, clutching the stinging limb to my side. I shouldn't feel the guilt slicing through my chest so keenly. The world shouldn't be spinning…

"I let you do that once," Damien murmurs. His face blurs in and out of focus, distorted by the blindfold. There's only shadow where his eyes should be. "I won't let it happen twice."

It's more than a warning. The weight of promised violence wraps around my neck like a noose, weighing me down until I hit the floor on my hands and knees.

My head throbs. The room splits in half, and suddenly, there are two of everything. Two tables. Two bottles of wine. Two mysterious, angry blind men sensing my motions through every sloppy sound I make.

"You're drunk," he declares on the cusp of a sigh.

"Liar," I croak, watching the light play over the floor. "I don't get drunk."

"Get up." He's in front of me, standing with his hand outstretched. From this angle, he's more imposing than he should be. A hulking monolith of a man.

I don't know why I reach for him this time, interlacing my fingers with his. He yanks me upright, but the world pitches beneath me, impossible to balance upon. My legs fold, but something catches me by the waist before I can fall. Something strong. Firm. Warm.

"I've got you." The voice sinks into my skin, resonating in my bones to spite me.

My palms flatten against the firm planes of his chest, and I push back but my legs buckle, making one thing clear: It's either him or the floor. Instinctively, my grip tightens over his forearms, rousing tightly coiled muscle that flexes beneath my fingers. God, he's *strong*—another realization that catches me off guard.

"Come." His breath fans my throat. "Sit."

He angles my body toward the couch and I can't stop the descent. Boneless, I land on the cushions width-ways, staring up at him.

"You drugged me." My words slur together, even as I know that my accusation isn't true. A drug would make me feel better, but I just feel numb.

"I warned you that the drink is stronger than what you're used to." The confidence with which he makes that assumption drenches me in foreboding.

"You don't know a damn thing about me."

"Don't I?" He cocks his head.

I shiver, bracing my hands against unyielding leather. He seems different from this angle. Bigger. To use his word, *imposing*.

"I know that every year on which just so happens to be your birthday, someone sends you the exact bottle of vintage

Romanée Conti that I've served you, but you never drink more than a few sips."

Shock grips my chest like a ruthless fist, squeezing the air from it. "You've been watching me." More than just watching. Peering into that black box that arrives every year to know the bottle. Unless he could decipher wine brands through touch alone, he had to have someone read him the label. "You're sick."

"I'm thorough, Ms. Thorne," he corrects without a shred of guilt or shame. "Know thy enemy."

"Enemy? So, you spied on me because you hate my father?"

But why tell me this now? Fear of the answer solidifies in my stomach and creeps up the back of my throat like bile. There has to be a reason.

"I always do my research, Ms. Thorne," he says. "I know you. I've watched you, as have so many others in your life."

Watched. Something about how he utters that word makes me roll onto my side and attempt to sit upright. I fail, smacking my head off the armrest as my ineffective limbs refuse to support my weight. "How? Why?"

"Curiosity. I want to be near enough to sense your reaction the day that all of your father's lies come crashing down around you." With that, he straightens his posture and elegantly extends his cane. "I'll have a car sent for you," he says as he starts for the door, tapping out a path.

"Wait!" I flail again in a desperate attempt to stand. Dizziness. The next second, my head is between my knees and my stomach is heaving.

I hear silence. Then footsteps coming closer. Closer…as the world spins faster and faster.

ELEVEN

I've never been hungover in my life, but I recognize the nauseating punishment my body enacts. College rumors don't do it justice; sobriety returns with a vengeance. Too exhausted to move, I just suck in air through my nose and attempt to decipher my surroundings.

I'm on my bed, I think. There is no mistaking the rasp of my custom sheets and the firmness of my mattress. How I got here. Well...

Those details are fuzzy. Alarmed, I blink my eyes open to make out the familiar comforts of my room. Gray daylight streams in through the window. Too bright. I groan and roll onto my side to escape it. Then I hear them.

Footsteps, soft and slow, approaching the bed. I jerk my focus toward the sound and spot him lingering just beyond my reach, dressed impeccably in a mixture of gray and black. In one hand, he's holding my favorite white mug. Steam wafts from the top and my nostrils wrinkle. Coffee.

"I recommend small sips," he says and sets the mug on my bedside table.

The resulting sound echoes like a gunshot, drawing a groan from my lips. My brain feels like a bowling ball bouncing off a skull made of tissue paper.

"What...what are you doing here?" Uh-oh. Something flakes off my chin as I speak. Dried. Crusty. I fight to lift my hand from the bed and swipe at my mouth with a trembling finger. Vomit.

"You were in no state to be left alone." He sounds disgusted by that fact and I shudder at what else I might have done to earn such a reaction. Not that I need to worry. Damien seems more than willing to tell me. "I didn't touch you more than necessary," he adds, a chilling preface.

I glance down and find my blouse partially undone. Someone wedged a damp cloth beneath the sleeve over my injured shoulder. My pants are still on, but my heels aren't. *Oh God*. The dried vomit takes on a different meaning.

"This is breaking and entering," I rasp. I try to sit up only to wind up on my back. The world won't stop spinning.

"It would be," Damien admits. "If you didn't invite me in."

Even drunk, I doubt I'd be so stupid. Rather than challenge him, I state the obvious. "Well, you can leave now."

He doesn't so much as flinch at the vitriol I spit his way. Instead, he reaches out, his fingers outstretched. I stiffen, choking on the air, but he grabs something from the nightstand near my bed. A handkerchief, one of his.

"Here." He drags the cloth against my cheek without warning. Without permission.

Sputtering, I cringe out of his reach. "Did you forget you're supposed to be blind?" I croak, eyeing his blindfold for any concealed slits.

"I can hear your breathing," he explains, letting the cloth fall onto the sheets. Sighing, he stands back and inclines his head toward the bedframe. "And I was listening from the other room. You haven't shifted much from the position I left you in."

Listening? Just how long has he been here, lurking outside my bedroom? I swallow hard and grasp the end of a sheet, dragging it over me as if the thin material can protect against his perception.

"Is that how you get by?" I wonder, annoyed that I sound more curious than mocking. "Remembering people's body positions?"

He tilts his head. "Well, I do paint the human body for a living. At least that's how the saying goes, isn't it?"

"Because you *don't* paint the human body for a living," I finish for him. Daddy used another word to describe his true profession. "You're a *criminal.*"

"Drink the coffee slowly," he tells me while withdrawing an object from the pocket of his slacks: the cane. Each delicate tap echoes as he heads for the door.

"Wait." Why I stop him, I don't know. His jaw clenches amid the snapping of teeth as he pauses near the doorway. "You said something last night." My heart squeezes as my brain sluggishly attempts to remember. What was it? "Something about my birthday," I add, fumbling with the words as they race from my mouth. "The wine. You knew. How?"

A simple shrugging of his shoulders and Damien becomes unreadable. "I don't remember anything of the sort, Ms. Thorne. Enjoy the rest of your day—"

"Wait." I manage to haul myself upright, using the pillow as a crutch. The words on the tip of my tongue don't leave it easily, almost as if every cell in my body resists the notion I stupidly propose. "So...so, when do we start?"

"Excuse me?" God, he sounds even more unnerving when he's confused. His voice dips an octave and his accent sharpens, honing every word into crisp syllables.

"When do we start?" I try to sound casual and fail. It would help if I didn't feel like roadkill. Or if this man weren't lying to me, withholding secrets about my own damn life.

I'll get to that, eventually. Until then...

"Painting me," I say, forging on. "I remember your terms." They were crystal clear: paralyzed by a drug, naked, and helpless at his mercy.

"And you agree to them?"

Do I? The ominous tingle running down my spine says no.

"If I *did*," I begin before he can say anything cutting, "when would we start?"

"This isn't a game."

I flinch. He's using that whip-like voice again, and my hungover brain struggles to impress upon me one key detail: He's a stranger in my house, able to navigate it with uncanny ease, especially for a blind man. He looks far too comfortable, lording over my master bedroom, which suddenly feels like a closet. I should be calling Daddy. The police. Anyone.

Not pushing his buttons, morbidly eager to learn more. He claims to know me, but I don't even have that luxury.

"I'm not playing." My voice almost sounds stable enough to back that statement. "So were you lying when you offered your services, or were you serious?"

I'm shivering. Only now am I aware of how my teeth are chattering. My blouse feels like tissue paper, ineffective against how my nipples have stiffened. Biology is betraying me in the worst possible way. Gritting my teeth, I drag the sheet farther over me.

He notices. The corner of his mouth twitches as if he's aware of everything I desperately seek to hide. The resulting expression isn't quite a smile or a frown. It's more terrifying than either.

It's curious.

"Yes or no," he demands, squaring his stance until he dominates my doorway and there's no way past him. I'm trapped. Physically. Figuratively. "I don't play with possibilities."

Suddenly, my lips feel dry enough that I run my tongue across them. Dehydrated flesh grates on the moist surface like sandpaper. Unfortunately, the pain doesn't reboot my common sense.

"Yes," I blurt as my stomach flips. "I'll do it. So, when do we start?"

"I should let you recover from last night," he says as if the idea just occurred to him.

As if I'm that fragile. That weak.

"No." I shift my weight and place my feet on the floor. "How about tonight?"

And this time, I'll corner him with questions he can't refuse. I'll get to the bottom of Damien. Even if…

My mind shies away from the train of thought. *Even if it kills me.*

"Hmm?" I prod when he doesn't answer. His jaw is tight again, his head still cocked like a predator avidly tracking his prey. Have I stumped the cool, collected Mr. Villa?

I suck in a breath when he nods. Apparently not.

"I'll consider it."

"C-consider it?"

He turns on his heel and exits my room without explanation, navigating toward what sounds like the foyer. "Have a good day, Ms. Thorne. Drink the coffee." He pauses, allowing the command to linger on the air. "I'll be in touch to inform you whether or not I'll humor your request."

"Humor?"

I hear the door open and close. By the time I manage to climb to my feet and stagger into the living room, he's gone. I race to the peephole and peer into the hall just in time to catch his silhouette flicker around the corner.

"Bastard," I hiss.

But as my voice echoes around me, I remember...

I'm alone again. With no one to stand between me and Simon. With no one there to see how my breathing becomes rapid and my body trembles. There's no time to regret the action. I already have the door open and I'm stumbling into the hall.

"Wait." I round the corner and find him standing before the elevator. A hiss of annoyance catches on the air. Yet he maintains the perfect poise of a gentleman.

"Can I help you, Ms. Thorne?"

"Why not just do it now and get it over with?"

He frowns at the suggestion. "I have other arrangements, and frankly, considering how much you drank, the alcohol is most likely still in your system. Mixing that with the drug I use can have dangerous side effects."

Fair enough. I take a step back and the elevator car arrives with a musical chime. I'm wringing my fingers together as he steps inside and feels along the wall panel for the ground floor button. It's the most convincing show of blindness from him yet. A minor hint of weakness. As the thought crosses my mind he nods, setting my body alight.

"Keep your phone close, Ms. Thorne. When I'm ready for you, I'll call. *Adiós.*"

The elevator doors slide neatly shut, closing him off. And suddenly my chest deflates as I exhale the breath I wasn't even aware of holding.

TWELVE

*D*amien can go to hell. One where he's forced to have *all* his senses to better contemplate his eternal suffering.

When I return to my room, I sample his coffee out of spite and almost spit it right back out. Damn. It's perfect, made exactly to my daily preference.

Too exact. Almost as if he's stood over my shoulder and watched me brew it for the past ten years, tweaking my habit to an art form. I take only one more sip before I toss the rest down the sink. Then I cross to my painting and observe it in the growing daylight despite how time stubbornly marches on. I'm late again. Or I would be if I were to go into the office.

Even the thought of returning now makes goosebumps prickle on the back of my neck. Not entirely because of what happened—but because of what hasn't.

No one's called reporting a break-in.

No police have asked about my attack.

The fact that someone could invade a public building in one of the busiest cities in the world without so much as a video popping up on social media is...

Chilling. Only Simon could pull it off—or someone far worse.

Rather than speculate, I call the building and confirm that Gus is alive and well at least.

"He had to leave early last night," the security supervisor explains. "Bad Chinese food."

Unease gnaws at my nerves as I linger in my apartment, sensing the flickering shadows from the corner of my eye. Every noise from the hall has me jumping, and my mind races with possibilities. Simon? Or Damien?

Which monster would I prefer? That's the true question and I hate that I can't answer it. My thoughts are too jagged to untangle.

In the hopes of finding some semblance of peace, I shed my rumpled clothing and climb into the shower of the guest bathroom, where everything is pristine and unbroken. God, I hate the woman watching me from the mirror. It's angled so that I have a clear view of myself, even while underneath the spray. Pale. Thin. Wide-eyed and haunted.

My right shoulder is bruised around the cut, which looks much worse when viewed from a distance. My lower lip is bitten, and even Damien couldn't clean up the worst of the vomit.

I'm disgusting, more grotesque than one of Sampson's paintings. All I need is a bed of blood-red roses to complete the aesthetic.

For now, my only accessory is the white towel I wrap around myself as I return to my bedroom and eye my closet critically. Every single item repels me. There's too much black. Too much tailored perfection. I spot a crumpled mass of wrapping paper and ribbon in the wastebasket near the foot of my bed and stiffen. How long has it been since I've worn that shade of purple?

My wardrobe doesn't contain the color at all. Maybe not since that day, all those years ago when I was dressed from head to toe in the shade. The best clothing Goodwill and Walmart could supply.

I wince. Bitter nostalgia strikes like an invisible fist to my stomach. I inhale raggedly and find something else to focus on. Like Damien. I left his sketch of me in the living room.

Still dripping wet and wearing only my towel, I head toward it. I'll rip it up this time and toss it into the trash, where it belongs.

Wait. My footsteps falter near the mouth of the hall before I even register my nostrils flaring. A faint, almost floral taint. Cologne? His scent announces his presence without my having to see him there, sitting on my couch, his posture imposingly erect.

"W-what are you doing here?" I mean to sound indignant. Not curious.

"Good evening." Damien inclines his head without facing me directly, almost as if he's riveted by the view from my window.

It's already late in the day. Indigo twilight washes over the horizon as a storm rages on. Thunder rumbles ominously. Lightning flashes. Funny. I didn't notice either until now.

"You weren't near your phone." His low tone perfectly mimics the muffled sounds of the storm.

He's wearing black again, the hypocrite—a suit tailored to perfection, crowned by a blood-red tie. Rather than the white cane, a real one made of carved wood leans against his knee. The handle of it is silver, shaped into the visage of a roaring lion.

"I wasn't?" I ask innocently. "I've been busy today."

"You haven't left this apartment." He sounds too damn sure of that, as if daring me to make the next leap in logic.

"Oh? And how would you know that?" I clutch my towel so tightly that my knuckles whiten. Things came back to me while I was in the shower. Memories I shied away from exploring in full, each one far too vivid to be from a nightmare. "Because you've been following me, haven't you? You knew what kind of wine I'd gotten. No one knows that—"

"I know everything about you," he says amid another foreboding strike of lightning. "Like the fact that you haven't expressed an interest in art a day in your life. That you manipulate lives for a living. That you and your father are one and the same."

"What the hell is that supposed to mean?"

He shifts in my direction and, God…I can feel his gaze piercing through me when it shouldn't.

"It means, if you want to play this game, I'll let you. To use your turn of phrase, let's get this over with." He lifts something clenched in his fist. A pen? No, it's too wide. Another flash of lightning illuminates the liquid inside and the long, thin tip encased in a plastic lid. A syringe. "I'll let you get a taste of what it's like to be truly helpless."

As if I don't already know how that feels. The storm building in intensity around us only compounds that fact. God, I just pray I won't panic, not around him. "Get out."

"*Sí.* As you wish." He rises to his feet, reaching for his cane. "Burn whatever information of mine Carla gave you. And you can keep the damn painting. I won't contact you again—"

"How long have you been watching me?" I blurt.

A denial should be his first instinct. Not a rich bark of laughter that resonates through my core, deeper than another roar of thunder. Strange. I should be having flashbacks about now. Vomit-inducing memories. Damien shouldn't be the one anchor tethering me to the present.

"Do you really want to know?"

"I… Do you stalk all of your potential subjects?" I counter.

"As I told you before, you are not a subject. *They* all concealed something worth learning."

Apparently, I don't.

"So, how does the injection work?" My throat goes dry as I eye the syringe still tucked into his free hand. The liquid catches what little light there is, giving off a faint shimmer. "You said it lasts for an hour."

"Typically. But one may perceive even a minute of being immobilized as an eternity."

He's not even being clever with the threats anymore. They spring from him like knives, conveying the one thing he seems hesitant to say directly. *You can't handle this.*

"So why do it?" I ask. "Someone doesn't have to be frozen for you to touch them."

He laughs again and the hairs on the back of my neck stand on end.

"If you have to ask, then you don't really understand my art as you claim to, *sí?*"

His words have me eyeing my painting again. Oh. As implied, the answer is in plain sight. There was no physical reason for his method. No, his motives are purely psychological. Every stroke captured the model's desperation. Her fear.

"Shouldn't you do this in your studio?" I ask. He doesn't have a briefcase with him, or canvas, or any other supplies.

"No," he says, his face illuminated by another flash of lightning. Thunder crashes, and the light in the room grows dimmer, swallowed by roving storm clouds.

I stiffen, ready for the fear. Visions of the forest. Simon. Anything but him.

Damien won't be banished so easily. He remains, tilting his syringe for my benefit. "This is merely for you to get a taste of just what you're requesting. I don't tailor my methods for anyone."

"And I'm not asking you to." Though why is that, exactly? I couldn't say.

My toes curl into the carpet as if to hinder every slow, careful step I take toward him. I stop just beyond his reach. If he comes for me, I can react. Or so I tell myself. "How do I know you won't kill me?"

"You don't." His voice falls flat.

"Fine, then." I tilt my chin and desperately try to combat the tremor in my voice. "What if you rape me while I'm like this?"

"Oh, but it wouldn't be rape, would it? In case you've forgotten my terms, you submit to me for however long you're under the drug's influence."

He sounds too damn smug. As if he's well aware of my pounding heartbeat. He wants to scare me—and he has.

"So...I'd have to trust you," I say, much more for my benefit than to score a reaction from him. But that word. It makes his upper lip pull back from his teeth.

"You'd *submit*."

"And everyone does this?" I shouldn't sound so hollow. So calm. Not when I can barely coax any air to go into my lungs.

He says nothing, letting me piece the answer together on my own. I'm not sure how long we stand there in silence before he finally taps the tip of his cane against the floor. "Goodnight, Ms. Thorne—"

"So we'll do it here, then?" I inch toward the couch. That strip of expensive leather and padding has never seemed so menacing. Damien's presence can turn everyday objects into new and unusual weapons of torture. I've walked this path a million times and never felt this sharp, aching thrill. "Or the bed?"

But I'm already sitting down, painfully aware of him behind me. He has yet to move away from the door. Maybe he won't. A sharp hiss is my only warning that once again I've foiled his expectations. For good or bad?

I'll worry about the answer later.

Minutes trickle by. Far too long. I'm freezing, still wearing only my towel. I should change. I start to rise and nearly jump out of my skin as a sharp thud shatters the silence, too close to be thunder.

"Sit," Damien commands.

From the corner of my eye, I see him lift his cane, the source of the sound. My legs fold like lawn chairs, depositing me right back down.

"S-should I get dressed?" I ask him.

"No." Slow, steady footsteps bring him to me.

I sense him, even before his hand settles over the back of the couch, searching. He swipes along the rim until he reaches my shoulder. With deliberate familiarity, he circles his fingers around the ridge of muscle and bone.

"It will be an intramuscular injection," he says. Warning me? "There will be some initial discomfort. Then numbness. You'll be able to breathe, but speaking will be difficult and I recommend against it. Do you have any medication allergies?"

I shake my head.

"Fine, then." He sounds resigned, more to his choice than my own. "Sit still. After this, I'll accept no change of heart. Do you agree to my terms?"

I should mull over the question, creating a dramatic silence worthy of the coward he thinks me to be. Mainly, I should cower and shiver beneath his touch. Not glisten with sweat I know he can feel.

"I agree," I say, copying his formal language. "I agree to your terms—" My voice ends in a hiss. Unseen, he must have injected me, right into the muscle of my upper arm.

"Discomfort" was an understatement. Burning fire consumes the muscle and spreads. I can feel it trickling into my bloodstream. My fingertips sear. My legs. My chest.

"It will take at least ten minutes for the full effect," Damien explains.

I hear a noise that sounds like his cane being propped against the back of the couch. Knuckles cracking next. Fabric rustling. His coat being shed, I realize as he circles around to face me.

He cocks his head, listening. I'm starting to recognize how he compensates for the loss of his vision—he's attentive. Calculating.

"S-should I lie down?" My voice comes out a scarce whisper, though I doubt the drug has taken effect this quickly. The sight of him has its own paralyzing effect. He's here, enforcing his presence in a way even Simon never has. I taste his flavor on my tongue and I'm not sure whether to spit him out or...

"It's up to you," he says, reinforcing his indifference to this entire situation. Poor man. I've confounded him—even though he's the one who broke into my home and put the choice before me in the first place.

My arm is starting to throb, so I decide to lie flat on my back with the site of the injection toward the open end of the couch. I've barely settled against the leather when I catch his frown.

"Remove the towel."

I can't silence my gasp. "H-how did you know?" Ignoring the fact that I mentioned getting dressed, I could be wearing pajamas for all he knew. No. Towel is far too specific. Just how long has he been here?

"You were in the shower," he says, only extending my curiosity. "You then went into the bedroom, but you didn't enter your closet. I didn't hear hangers being moved. Or drawers being opened. You take at least ten minutes to dress normally, but you were out in three."

He recited such a methodical list for a reason. To inflict the most terror. And he has.

My eyes go to the door. I can still move my limbs. Long enough to get help? I brace one foot against the floor, preparing to stand.

"How long have you been watching me? How? Do you always come into my house while I'm—"

"You should conserve your energy, Ms. Thorne. We're already at two minutes."

"Then admit it," I hiss through gritted teeth. "How long have you been stalking me?"

"I think a better question is: Who *else* might be watching you, Juliana Thorne?"

I flinch at the insinuation. He knows of the wine, but is he aware of who sent it and why? Does he know about Simon?

"As for why, it's simple: Because I can. I've had a window into your life you couldn't realize in your nightmares."

My fingers clutch the couch on either side of me, readying for the moment I decide to run. Which is exactly what he wants me to do. He's goading me on purpose. Scaring me. I should damn well take the hint. I shouldn't question.

"If I'm so uninteresting to you, then why waste your precious time and resources following my *boring*, predictable life?"

He frowns. "I'll tell you why: Heyworth Thorne."

"My father?"

"*Sí.* Don't sound so surprised, Juliana. I'm sure you've gotten enough reminders this week alone as to why someone might have a grudge against your father. Why *I* might..."

Ah. A not-so-subtle insinuation that he's spied on me in my office as well. "So you know about the messages I've gotten. Friends of yours?"

He chuckles. "I prefer to send more...direct messages, Ms. Thorne." His fingers flex at his sides, drawing my attention. I see a sudden image of him hunched over a sheet of paper, channeling his rage into vivid sketches.

"What do you have against my father?" I'm merely stalling now.

I'm not as naïve as Mr. Villa appears to think, and the recent news coverage merely exposed an open secret: Daddy isn't as perfect as he pretends to be. Neither is his judgment.

"Did he convict you of too many traffic violations or something?"

"Too many traffic violations…" He laughs again, more deeply than before. The sound serves as a chilling foil to another crack of thunder, louder than all those before it. "You should really read a newspaper article, Ms. Thorne. It's right there in black and white."

Ah, but wasn't he the one who spelled it out for me? I'm sheltered. Innocent. A fucking pathetic coward. Daddy has his own demons to deal with, and I've been more than willing to let him battle them alone.

"Enlighten me, then," I demand. Forming the words takes more effort than it should. The clock on the wall reveals why. Seven minutes.

"No." He crosses to me like a snake, sensing out my position through motion and sound. His hand reaches out, his fingers searching until they find my chin. "I'll let you think about it, Juliana." He tilts my head back and my limp muscles are no match. I can't even raise a finger against him. "I'll let you play with every dark scenario that might flit around that simple mind of yours. You worried that I might kill you. Rape you. But do you know what I *really* want to do to you?" He leans in close, his breath hot on my skin.

My throat refuses to form words. Even a gasp. All I can do is stare.

"I'm going to let you sit here in the fucking dark. Alone." He drags his thumb in a cruel imitation of a caress as terror locks me in a vise-grip. "Do you know the real reason why I stayed with you last night? You *begged* me to. Nothing terrifies you more than silence. The darkness. The emptiness..."

He's lying. I cling to that hope, even as the repressed memories from last night flutter to the surface. Thrashing on sweat-soaked sheets, seeing Simon in the shadows. Grasping someone's hand so tightly that I could sense the bones and ridges that made up their fingers. Touching skin so soft that I could tear it. Croaking a single word over and over. *Stay. Stay. Stay. Stay.*

My eyes blink rapidly—the only physical act I have control over.

"Enjoy your night, Ms. Thorne." He steps back, silhouetted by the storm raging behind him, and moves beyond my line of sight.

"D-don't..." I have to shove the word off my tongue, my chest heaving with the effort.

He'll leave anyway. I wait for the sound of the door slamming shut. For the silence that's become the soundtrack of my adult life.

I wait.

And he lingers, lurking just beyond the reach of my peripheral vision. Air trickles in and out of paper-thin lungs. The clock tells me why; it's beyond ten minutes. My muscles and nerves have become deaf to any command my brain issues. I can't even turn my head. Only my ears aid in sensing just where he is. Paces from the couch. Maybe in that exact spot where the carpet turns to the tile of the kitchen. From there, and with his height, he'll have the perfect view of me. Sprawled upright, trapped beneath the towel. Without my fingers to support it, the terrycloth rides dangerously low. And yet…

It's not my body he seems to be after.

My heart lurches as his footsteps return, drawing closer. At first, I fear he'll stay where I can't see him. But no. He enters my line of sight, sans his cane…and I shouldn't be relieved. Not given the way he looks. Jaw clenched. Furrowed lines around the edges of his blindfold.

Panting. The sound comes from me, clashing with the muted sounds of rain and thunder. It picks up, feathering into breathless gasps as he advances step by step. He hunts me through the act alone, his head cocked, his posture rigid.

I nearly jump out of my skin when his finger brushes my cheek. He wasn't lying. I feel everything. The softness of his skin. The faintest slickness of sweat, even though I'm freezing. He traces a path to my mouth and hovers his thumb over my parted lips, sensing how they quiver.

His other hand comes slowly, almost reluctantly, to seek out my forearm. Then my collarbone. Finally, he finds the edge of my towel and sinks his fingers into the material. He tugs it away and my lips flutter open around a gasp.

Helpless like this, I have no comparison to any other moment in my life. Simon made me feel small and cornered, like a mouse, always running on a wheel that would never move. Damien, in this moment, makes me feel like...

Prey. Only he's a disinterested predator. I'm more helpless before him than I've ever been around any other monster— even the one who tried to kill me. Yet he controls how much of me he wants to see. My lips at the moment. Then the tender, bony ridge of my rib cage where my heartbeat can be felt the most.

Watching him stand over me is too damn surreal. So I force my eyes shut and listen, copying how he must sense me. I'm nowhere near as warm as he is, and my hands aren't halfway as soft.

My pulse quickens, and I can almost visualize the sound pulsating through his fingertips, giving me away. Touch feels far more penetrating than sight ever could. He can feel what my facial expression wouldn't reveal. My fear. Terror. Curiosity?

The other women, the ones so intriguing that he rendered them motionless to decipher their secrets. I bet he explored them far more intimately than he does me. Good. I should count my blessings. Thank God he isn't interested in peering too deeply beneath my shell.

Wrong. His main goal seems to be to circumvent my expectations at every turn. The hand he has on my chest curls, cupping more flesh, kneading it just to the point of roughness. To hear me scream. As easily as he deciphers me, I'm finding that I can do the same to him. He wants me to protest, so I make a concerted effort to say nothing.

I don't gasp. I don't whimper. I don't even breathe.

I simply feel, locked inside my own body. Now seems like the wrong moment to realize that he's the first man to ever touch me like this. Really touch me. Naked flesh beneath roaming fingers. Should I feel robbed of some precious moment? My future lover has been beaten to this intimate discovery. He'll have to be content with whatever Damien leaves untouched.

Which will be nothing.

Something in the air changes. Thunder surges as if feeding off the emotion conveyed in the thumb he wedges between my lips to pry them apart. Determination. Morbid curiosity. How far can he push me?

Another searching path of his hand down my chest conjures up the answer I don't want to face. Too far. He's closer, his footsteps landing in menacing tandem. I hear his breath catch on a resigned sigh. He'll play this stupid game I've set in motion. He'll play to win. The hand on my chin curls, cupping my face fully, tilting it back

"Are your eyes open? I'm assuming they aren't," he says, employing that uncanny knowledge of me to unsettling effect. "You always run when you're frightened. Cower." His thumb strokes upward, stopping short of my eyelid. "Open them."

He's right. Playing the role of a frightened mouse is the role I play the best. I've grown accustomed to fear's bitter sting. How it grapples for control from my limbs and paralyzes me more than this drug ever could. I should feel it now, the icy tendrils of terror. Hell, I welcome it.

But he's wrong.

I keep my eyes shut, feeding off the tension building in his fingertips. He senses my disobedience without ever having to see it.

"Remember your word, Juliana Thorne," he warns, issuing another callous stroke to my cheek. "I know honor is a murky concept in your family, but you promised your submission. Open. Your. Eyes."

Another crack of thunder reinforces the malice in his tone. But I keep myself blind. For the first time in my life, it isn't because I'm afraid of what I'll see. I know the sight awaiting me: a stern-faced villain bolstered by crackling lightning and distracting shadows. Deciphering him through touch is ten times more disorienting. There are no snap judgments I can make. Just slow deliberation based off the sparks ignited in my skin wherever his touch roams.

Daddy's method won't help me here. Damien requires a new form of deduction. Like the fact that even when he boldly grazes his hand over my breast there's no real malice in it. The thumb braced between my teeth reveals more. It stiffens, capturing the gasp choked from my throat. At first, he presses harder, relishing the perceived triumph. Not even a second later, he withdraws the pressure.

"Apparently, you still believe this to be a game."

I've never known such a thick, impenetrable silence before. Even the weather seems to pause its assault, riveted by the man whose anger bastes my skin with every breath. Another harsh stroke along my chin tilts my face toward the palm of his hand. With no control, I'm at his mercy. He could toy with me like a rag doll, or worse. But no, Damien's style is more psychological than anything.

"I think you've been alone too long, Juliana," he tells me, his voice grated. I suspect he knows damn well just how long it's been. "A good, wholesome woman such as yourself shouldn't be reacting to me."

Apparently, he doesn't know me as well as he thinks. I've never been good, always pretending. Wholesome is a term that best applies to the extent of my lies. Whole. Consuming.

"Are you that desperate for…" He trails off, letting my imagination run wild to fill in the gap.

His attention drifts lower, more slowly than before. Spreading fingers and dull nails perform their search with more intent. Friction sparks. Fire follows. Locked in place, my muscles can't even shudder beneath the violation. I've never wanted to recoil so badly in my life. I've never been so attuned to my body's reaction to anything. Not Simon. Not anyone.

"Open your eyes, Juliana." He's closer. His words strike my lower jaw like fire.

My ears pick up the slight ambiance they normally wouldn't. The crunch of fabric conformed to a muscular body. The creaking of my floor. Rain lashing glass. The high-pitched, breathy noises coming from my throat.

He must crouch to his knees, crushing the carpet beneath his bulk. The leather hisses, presumably brushed by the fabric of his shirt. Those hot fingers drift lower...

"Open your eyes."

It should be impossible for him to know that I haven't. Almost as impossible as it should be for me to sense the hard swallow he takes. A low sound nips at the air. Thunder? No. It's too deep. Too masculine. Too damn close.

His dominant hand has never left my face. His thumb performs a near constant stroking, up and down. Down and up. Quicker each time, the next brush more menacing than the last. Gritted teeth create an ominous warning amid the backdrop of yet another flash of lightning. This one so bright that I can see it, brilliant silver against my eyelids.

"Open." His voice rumbles against my ear. His thumb flicks my cheek, while his other hand becomes even bolder.

"N-no..." Only God knows how I manage to rasp out the word. I'm still paralyzed. Speaking feels like trying to scream with an iron weight pressing down on my chest. But he makes it possible. So confident that he knows me so damn well. "Want...to...feel..."

He laughs. Such a terrible, violent sound. My toes would curl if they could. Instead, my mouth waters and I know he can sense the moisture against his thumb. It returns to its position between my lips, testing what little control I still have over my jaw.

"Feel?" His touch moves lower.

More sparks. More fire—no, *explosions* set off beneath my skin.

"I can make you feel a million things, Juliana Thorne," he promises. Dark things. Awful things. His hand slides between my legs, giving me a mere taste of what his threat conveys.

And I choke on it.

Too much. Too much heat ripping through me. Too little control of my body. All I can do is breathe in and out. Noisily. Pained. His thumb is a rigid anchor and my tongue seeks it out, desperate to retaliate in some way.

"Open your eyes. Though perhaps I should do the honors, figuratively speaking?" He drags my legs apart as he speaks.

While I'm blinded, the sensations of slick leather and silken fingers resonate tenfold. Cool air assaults heated flesh. I suck in a breath. Too sensitive. My eyelids flutter. Make it stop.

Never have this end.

"Your father is a man of contradiction," Damien grits out. Something brushes my earlobe, imparting a tendril of alarm. Moist. Soft. His lips? His mouth, lowered so close that I feel every lash of his tongue as he speaks. "In public, he pretends to be the beacon of justice, but in private? He hides and obfuscates whatever he can. He's had all of his past records erased. Wiped clean. Did you know that? Not the good cases of course, but the others... Now, be the good little girl you are for everyone else and open. Your father could order you to jump off a fucking cliff and you would, wouldn't you?"

Probably.

The heart-stopping fall would be preferable to this; at least I'd know what to expect. I'd see the bottom in advance. I'd never have the chance to regret my decision for very long.

But this...

Lightning strikes. Thunder rumbles, and all the while, Damien breathes his hate into my skin. There's no clear line of sight to the end of my fall. I could be suspended for ages. Or hit the ground without warning.

"Open."

I don't bother denying him out loud. *I can't.* His thumb twists inside my mouth until the nail grazes my tongue. Boom! Flash! He's created his own storm inside me.

"I don't particularly care to molest you, Ms. Thorne." He almost sounds convincing. If only his accent didn't wrap around that little word—*molest*—and strangle it beyond recognition.

I know the word he substituted it for. Destroy.

I don't particularly care to destroy you, Ms. Thorne. But I will.

The hand between my legs twitches in warning as his voice straddles that guttural octave. "Open your goddamn eyes."

"N-no—"

Inferno. He must have anticipated my response, because silken fingers cup me without hesitation. Ruthlessly. My thoughts scatter at the contact. Total shutdown. What little air I have in my lungs escapes in a rush. Every nerve I possess overloads and then comes back online, one after the other. Sensation first. Then the parts of my brain capable of interpreting it. Heat. Fire. Sweltering. Raw. Skin. Soft. Everywhere, everywhere, *everywhere.*

Motion rustles near my earlobe as he murmurs something unintelligible. *Open.* I register a ragged inhale. Sharp exhale. Then he growls, "*Mierda.* What game are you playing?"

As if I'm the one who wields the control. I wish I were. I'd push him off. Run away. I'd cower and hide like he wants me to.

"Open," he snarls.

But the darkness is addicting. Beneath its veil, I can interpret more of him than ever before. He's closer, leaning his weight toward my position. What must be his torso brushes the tips of my knees, not quite forcing its way between them. But almost. Heat fans my neck in tandem with his breathing. Harsh. Slowed. He's grappling for calm, something I doubt I'll ever find again.

"For the last time…open your eyes."

I don't. He retaliates.

Only the power of my imagination allows me a vague inclination of what he does next: slide a finger inside me. My frozen muscles don't offer him any slack. He has to force it. I have to feel it. Friction—bitter, searing friction. Tightness. Closeness. A feeling beyond fire or inferno. A nuclear blast.

A strangled cry crawls up my throat, but I barely hear myself beneath his grunted exclamation.

"*Qué mierda*!"

Doused. He pulls back so suddenly that that's what it feels like: being drenched in ice water and left to freeze.

His mouth remains near my ear, however, his thumb trembling against my tongue. "You're a virgin."

He sounds incredulous. He sounds...furious?

I don't know whether to lie or admit the truth. So I say nothing. But he wins. The breadth of his confusion feels far too great to experience through feel alone. I have to open my eyes and see his clenched, disgusted expression for myself.

He's closer than I thought, hunched against me, his hand still between my legs, his face almost parallel to mine. There's no avoiding the path my eyes take. Even blindfolded, his features form a beautiful silhouette in the dark—but make a terrifying contrast when lightning flashes.

"Are you?" he demands. Another searching thrust of his thumb fractures my attention. Can't focus. "Too tight," he grates, speaking more to himself than me. "Have to be."

I bite my tongue and he draws back, rising to his feet. The loss of his heat deals a harsher blow than it should. Cold air cruelly replaces him as he starts to pace. One of his hands tears through his hair. The same one he had inside me. The nails on it assault his scalp, ripping strands of ebony hair from his neat ponytail. In place of *me*.

I'm the real target of his rage. To prove it, his head swivels in my direction and I sense his focus on my fingers. Looking down, I see why. They're flexing against the leather, straining for leverage as the hand on the clock inches minutes past an hour.

But I'm a long way from moving. If anything, the slight tease of freedom is a million times worse. I'm not so helpless, but still at his mercy. Still vulnerable to the threat he voiced. *I'll leave you here in the dark.*

"D-don't. P-please!" The plea scrapes my throat as he stalks past the couch, beyond my sight. With my eyes wide open, it's harder to assume what he's doing. Wood drags across carpet. Fabric swishes through the air. Footsteps angrily approach my door. "W-wait—"

"Once upon a time, you were left alone in the dark." There's what could be mistaken for pity in his voice. Almost—and it unnerves me like nothing else. "Afraid. Abandoned. In so many ways, you will always be that little girl."

The door opens. Slams shut. Rain hammers against my windows, drowning out my rapid breathing.

Shadows loom across the floor. He must have disabled my automatic lights somehow, because they don't come on no matter how my fingers flutter. I'm frozen. For one minute. Two minutes…

There's no bluffing on his part. I'm swallowed by the silence. The loneliness. It circles me like a predator, waiting for the right moment to strike. It comes as lightning illuminates the sky and thunder reverberates through the very foundation of my building. Panic.

Bit by bit—cell by fucking cell—movement returns.

But all I can do is scream and remember.

Simon says…

THIRTEEN

You're never lonely with a...

"Smile so hard and you might hurt yourself!" Sharla from accounting makes the assessment as she drops a stack of documents onto my desk.

My mouth practically waters at the prospect of more work. These will take hours, if not days to review. Less time to think. When I swipe my hand longingly over the pages, the perky blond raises an eyebrow.

"You must be having the best day ever. You haven't stopped smiling since you came in."

She's right. I haven't. My mouth aches with the effort it takes to maintain my flawless expression. I'm happy, all right. So damn happy.

"Thank you." I beam wider as Sharla saunters off and closes the door of my office behind her.

The moment she's gone, I lift a mug from the corner of my desk and drain it in one go. The liquid running down my throat isn't coffee—the one risk in my façade I'm willing to take. As they have since the moment I woke up, memories from last night play tauntingly across the inside of my skull and only alcohol can counter them. *This* sinister brand, to be exact.

Maybe I'm as much of a masochist as I am a coward. The bitter taste serves as a harsh reminder of just what Damien is capable of. Stalking. Drugging. Abandoning.

It took two hours after he left for me to regain control of my limbs and crawl into my bedroom. I only had enough strength left to switch on every damn light before a pounding headache drove me beneath the blankets and into a dreamless sleep—a quick Google search revealed a headache could be a potential side effect of succinylcholine. So that was that. He hadn't poisoned me at least, and somehow, I woke up in time to hobble into my closet and get dressed for work.

But something else he said makes me compile another search, and the results are more puzzling. Legal cases have never interested me before—not even my father's before he took the bench. A cursory search reveals a few of his landmark cases as a defense attorney, but little else.

Erased, Damien said. In fact, the only thing even remotely out of place is a single headline from over twenty-one years ago reading "**All Charges Dropped Against Child Murder Suspect.**" My father was briefly mentioned as the defense attorney, but the police apparently had no solid evidence and the suspect was never named. Nothing nefarious in that. Still, the topic of murder makes me shudder. Could that case be why Heyworth Thorne picked me, of all children, to adopt? Misplaced guilt?

Perhaps Damien thinks that fact might shock me. Oh no, my father didn't happen across me by chance, but he sought me out because my case paralleled another he'd worked on. How evil.

But the bastard is a liar. And he's ruthless. There were some lines even Simon hadn't crossed. I asked my questions last night, but this morning brought my answers: Damien is more than just creepily intuitive.

After fishing out the bottle of wine hidden under my desk, I fill my mug to the brim and down half of it before focusing my attention on the small object beside my computer keyboard. It's black and square-shaped, and it resembles an earpiece one might use for telephone calls.

Or spying.

I found it tucked discreetly near the bulb of my desk lamp this morning. I didn't have to look hard—it was almost as if whoever had placed it there *wanted* me to find it. For all I know, there could be more. Or a camera watching me from some unseen corner.

If so, I give my audience a damn good show. I smile until my jaw feels liable to fracture from the stress. I comb through my work at record speed. I even deign to join the others for drinks after.

Anything to ignore the persistent reminders of last night. My throbbing arm. My worn, broken fingernails. The slight ache between my legs...

Stop. No fear. No flashbacks. He won't win again. Determined, I keep on smiling. At the bar, I buy a round of drinks for everyone and take the first shot to come my way, pushing the thoughts back.

When the last tab is finally paid, I enter a town car alone and direct the driver toward the Harrison Hotel rather than the Lariat. I book my usual suite and toy with the idea of buying a bottle of wine from the downstairs bar. Something cheap enough to make a rich bastard choke.

Somewhere during the trip down the hallway, I lose my nerve and enter my room painfully sober. Groaning, I strip my coat, leaving it by the door. Then I switch the light on and head straight for the bed, intending to sink beneath the covers and into oblivion.

A shadow catches my eye at the exact moment an ominous scent floods my nostrils: *roses.* My footsteps falter, forcing me to clutch the wall for balance. I'm just paces from the door, but escape feels miles away.

"Wait," my intruder commands. He stands near a massive window with his back to me.

I tense. He's dressed in black, accented with gray tonight. Like always, the blindfold is tied neatly over the ridge of a black ponytail. In any other circumstance, I might consider him appealing.

As it stands now, I can't read the bastard at all.

Daddy's tried-and-true method fails me thoroughly where Damien is concerned. The man wears no mask. There's nothing to judge. Just plenty to hate.

"Get the hell out." I'll beat him to the punch. My fingers swipe at the door but tremble too badly to grip the handle. I knot them into fists and inhale. *Get a hold of yourself.* "Now," I huff between ragged breaths, "before I call the police—"

"I'd like to suggest that we renegotiate our previous agreement." He's too calm. Even though I know he can hear me pawing at the door again.

Yes. I get it open. All I have to do is throw myself over the threshold and run.

"If you're still willing to agree to my terms, that is."

"Your what?" I snap. How dare he keep talking as though this were a normal meeting. A normal day. As if we were normal goddamn people.

"My terms."

"Terms?" I parrot him while looking over my shoulder. "Did they include leaving me incapacitated?"

And alone. In the dark. Something he himself mocked me for fearing. Not that it matters. He can play silly mind games all he wants—just as long as he keeps his toys to himself.

"By the way, I found one of your little spies." I expect him to at least flinch in some semblance of guilt. The bastard doesn't even sigh. "Right. You called me boring, but how interesting must *your* life be if you decide to listen to mine every fucking day, huh?"

Oh, because he *has* been listening.

"Please close the door, Ms. Thorne. Then we can discuss why I'm here." He doesn't sound so suave anymore. The catch in his voice prompts a manic surge in my heartbeat— but out of fear or triumph?

My, my, it looks like I've annoyed the unflappable Mr. Villa.

Good.

"I don't think so." I pull the door open wider. "I want everyone in this whole damn building to hear. Come for me and I'm screaming." Which will be quite the feat considering I'm barely speaking louder than a whisper. "Now, get out—"

"I wanted to...apologize."

I tense, waiting for the laugh. The cruel punchline. The mocking taunt. Panic sweeps through my veins when seconds pass without him performing either act.

"Most men send flowers to do that," I croak. "They don't break into people's private rooms. Though, with your affinity for destroying things, maybe you should stick to mangling rose petals. By the way, I looked into my father's record as you suggested."

He inclines his head. "Oh?"

"Congratulations. I've learned that he's a good man who's done his best to right his past mistakes. Anything else? Any more nasty hints you want to drop? No? Then get the hell out—"

"You sound healthy enough. The drug can sometimes cause lasting fatigue. You've recovered?"

He's doing it again. Displaying that terrible knack of humanity like a switchblade, shoving it discreetly where it can penetrate the deepest. He doesn't *really* care. Despite the way his head tilts, putting his ear in the prime position to catch my reaction: gritted teeth and rapid breaths.

"I recovered, all right. I had plenty of time while I was *crawling* to my room alone, in the dark, to reflect upon why I should listen to my father the next time he warns me about a dangerous, psychopathic—"

"And here I was, assuming that you had such a wonderful day." He cocks his head with devastating candor, his voice ice cold. So much for playing contrite. "Whatever happened to your smile?"

Bastard. Finding his little toy was one thing. Hearing him parrot such casual banter from my daily life is another entirely. I'm shaking, and this time, I have no trouble stepping into the hall.

"Goodnight, Mr. Villa," I spit out without looking back. "Enjoy the view. And from now on, you can take your so-called apology and shove it up your ass."

Such a callous statement would demand a slow, collected walk to go with it. Any other night I'd try, but I can't reach the elevator fast enough. Once outside, I chase down a cab —but rather than the Lariat, I have the driver take me to the one place I instinctively know Damien won't dare venture.

I go home to Heyworth Thorne.

And I intend to tell him everything.

FOURTEEN

I open my eyes to a perfect bedroom ripped from the pages of a home and garden magazine. One of those glossy editions featuring rooms resembling a dollhouse setup more than anything people actually live in. This dollhouse family loves their pastels: lemon-yellow walls reflect the bright sunlight streaming in through a bay window.

Tucked beneath a matching duvet, I barely slept. Though not for lack of trying.

My cage was carefully prepared in advance, courtesy of Diane, Daddy's second wife. I recognize her handiwork; she must have come into the room last night, fished an ornate box from the antique wardrobe in the corner and withdrew enough nightlights to fill every single outlet. Then she switched on the white noise machine hidden behind a potted fern to block out any hint of an approaching thunderstorm.

She even left clothing out for me: jeans and a simple blouse —both black and unassuming. After getting dressed, I make a show of yawning as I descend the steps to an audience of one.

"It's not like you to pop in so late, sweet pea."

Daddy stands in the doorway of the kitchen, sipping coffee from a mug while wearing his trademark grin. Ours mirror each other, in fact: pearly white and perfectly straight. But he strays from the script; his eyes narrow and give me an anxious sweep.

"Is everything all right?" He doesn't require a drug to see through my defenses.

"Everything's fine," I lie, straight-faced. "It's just… I wanted to check up on you."

"Oh, really?" He sighs. "I may be getting on in years, darling, but I'm not oblivious. Now, don't lie to me. You saw the news last night, didn't you?"

I say nothing as my heart hammers away in my chest.

"I don't want you to worry," he continues. "The police will find out who is behind these horrendous crimes. The perpetrator won't get away."

The sarcasm in his tone makes me suspect that he has an idea of who that perpetrator might be. "You think Damien Villa is behind this?"

"Not him directly," he admits without an ounce of hesitation. "His family perhaps. His brother. They're dangerous, Juliana. But I don't want to discuss this now. Come, I bet you're starving."

He inclines his head for me to follow him into the kitchen, where a steaming plate of breakfast is already waiting for me, courtesy of his chef, Craig. Daddy takes the seat beside me and fishes a cigar from his pocket.

I glance at the clock. "Isn't it a little too early for that?"

Rather than answer me, he takes a puff of the cigar and inhales the smoke so deeply that he coughs.

I make a show of fussing over him, patting his back. "Daddy, you know this isn't good for you—"

"I increased the guard duty I have on you, at least until the conference," he admits, in between two more puffs. "I told them to give you your space, but they're alert. Have you noticed a difference at all?"

Difference? Yes, I have. Primarily, a deranged lunatic strolling into my home like he owns it.

"Y-yes." By some miracle, I keep my flawless smile intact. "I've felt safer."

"Good. Good." Daddy sighs. Apparently, I'm not the only one exhausted by these past few days.

"What's wrong?"

When I shift closer to him, he slaps his hand over the newspaper lying nearby. I only catch a glimpse of the headline before he rolls it up and tosses it aside: **Borgetta Prosecutor Found Dead of Suspected Suicide.**

I reach for my untouched mug of coffee and gulp a mouthful of liquid to disguise the shudder ripping through me. Another murder. Could Damien or his family truly be behind it?

I don't know and that terrifies me.

"How are the campaign preparations going?" I ask, desperate to change the subject. Looking at Daddy's tortured expression, I realize I've stepped on a landmine instead.

"Slow," he replies. "It seems my prior donors have been discouraged from continuing their contributions."

He doesn't have to say why: because of Damien.

The man isn't done "discouraging" me, either. My cell phone rang once in the early hours of the morning, displaying a message from an unknown number. I deleted it without bothering to listen—I have no proof the call came from him—but it fit his MO.

He merely wanted to reinforce his presence and drill one fact into my skull: He can always find me.

"Juliana?" Daddy covers my hand with his. "Are you all right?"

"Fine." I widen my smile only to belatedly remember the topic at hand. "I'm so sorry, Daddy. Discouraged... What do you mean?"

"Intimidated." He scowls into his mug. "It seems the bastard is determined to thwart my campaign before it can even begin."

A preemptive strike. Like nipping a wayward rose in the bud—or poisoning a potential threat with oleander. Swift and malicious with an unmistakable artistic flair. The man truly is a sadist.

"But why?" I swallow hard, hating the hoarseness in my voice. "Why is he doing this?"

"Oh…" He shakes his head, but I don't miss how his eyes cut to the discarded newspaper and back. "It's this damn mess with the Borgetta case. What happened to his brother was unfortunate but—"

"His b-brother?" Coffee sprays from my mouth, splattering the table. I cough to disguise my shock. Then I snatch up a napkin and dab at what I can reach. "I-I mean…oh, now I understand."

Of course. How could I be so fucking stupid? Damien's brother was at the center of the case my father tried, and all of his cruel taunts make sense now: *I watched you. Know thy enemy. You're just like your father…*

"They're all criminals, that family. I don't give a damn what anyone says. The other brother, Mateo, has been rumored to belong to a Columbian cartel, and Damien pretends to be above it, but he's a part of it too."

Daddy's never sounded like this before. Callous. A sneer contorts his features; he's a stranger. A heartbeat later, he squeezes my hand and chortles, his charming self in the blink of an eye. "But I don't want you to worry about this, sweet pea. Enjoy your breakfast—"

"Daddy, can I ask you something?" The question is out before I can even process it.

"Anything, darling."

"Why are some of your past cases struck from the record?" It should sound so harmless in hindsight. So harmless and innocent that my father nearly jumps out of his skin.

"Juliana…" His tone hardens in a way I've rarely heard. He spoke to criminals like this, seen only in clips of his glory days sometimes plastered over the news in conjunction with the current headlines. "Were you looking for a case in particular?"

"No," I admit. Only now I wonder if I should be. If Damien was more than planting suspicions in my skull for the hell of it. "I was just curious. Looking for examples of all of the good you've done to help combat the press."

"Old cases get cleared from the records all of the time," he says. "I'll leave you to your breakfast."

He leaves, taking his cigar with him. Presumably to return to his office and fume.

The moment he's gone, I grab the newspaper he left behind and read it surreptitiously from under the table. As expected, the headlining story contains even more scandal.

The man who prosecuted the Borgetta murder case ten years ago—a man with emergent ethical complaints related to evidence tampering—was found dead of a gunshot wound to the head last night. Self-inflicted, according to the police.

Daddy's sudden interest in my security makes sense now. He's afraid.

Though maybe he should be. I run my fingers along my shoulder, struck by a sudden realization: Simon isn't the only monster bold enough to hunt me these days. Could I be the star of the next grisly headline? My stomach churns and breakfast becomes an afterthought.

If Damien Villa is behind these murders, it wouldn't be much of a leap. Given the morbid nature of his art, there's no telling where a man like him would draw the line from paralyzed subjects to lifeless victims. Murder could run in the Villa family. Though how would I know. I never had siblings—the closest thing I might compare that affection to is my friendship with Leslie.

And I'm still suffering the consequences of failing her.

How far might someone go for their brother?

While I haven't read too much into the case overturning the Borgetta conviction, I'm inclined to believe my father's judgment.

After all, some display their darkest impulses for the world to see.

Like Damien's art...

I shiver, recalling how illustrated, hollow eyes held me captive. In the model's painted gaze, I found terror, fear, passion, life. Those elusive traits a certain artist claimed I didn't possess.

Just how long has he been watching me to know as much? I left his bug in my office drawer—a rather stupid hiding place in retrospect—but something warns me there are more. In the boardroom? In the hallway? The lobby? I name every location I can while avoiding the most obvious target.

The thought of Damien listening in on my private moments is enough to drive me upstairs, into the shower. I turn the water as hot as it can go and scrub my skin raw. Then I redress in Diane's borrowed clothing, sequester myself in the guest bedroom, and do the one act that Simon, after all these years, never made me do. I call the office and I take a week off work, citing the drama around my father's overturned cases.

"I just need a few days," I lie.

When I return downstairs and join my father in the great room, I intend to announce my desire to spend the rest of the week. As Daddy angrily flips through the channels to avoid the news stations, the words are poised on the tip of my tongue. *You need me here.*

Try as I might, I can't spit them out. Seven days is more than twice what Simon ever took from me at one time. I've already conceded my life to one dangerous man. Psychopath or not, there is no way in hell I'll surrender more of myself to another.

Emboldened, I tell Daddy goodbye and have his driver return me to town. On the way there, I call the management of the Lariat and demand my suite be searched upon my arrival. For good measure, I request an armed escort.

Two can play the surveillance game.

Flanked by a guard twenty minutes later, I feel confident enough to face Damien head-on. Once I reach my door, I boldly swipe my keycard and step inside. Only to suffocate.

Roses.

Exotic masculinity.

Intimidation.

My nostrils flare, catching every scent before my other senses even register the danger.

"Wait, miss!" The guard grabs my shoulder, making me trip over the threshold. He mutters something I don't hear.

I'm too busy hallucinating. Somehow, I manage to choke out a statement of my own. "What in the hell?"

I step farther into the foyer without waiting for an answer. My eyes blink, unwilling to register the scene before them.

Someone drenched my gray color scheme in a bloody shade of red. It's everywhere. Rose petals, to be exact. Hundreds coat the floor in a haphazard spread. Menacing enough on their own, the mutilated buds are merely the icing on the cake of unease my tormentor sought to deliver.

I don't realize that I've circled around to my coffee table until I'm standing before it, a trail of crushed petals in my wake.

There, lying on the exact spot where I was the other night, is a square object wrapped neatly in crimson paper. A black bow gives it a wicked finish. Anticipation and sweat slick my palms, and it's suddenly impossible to breathe.

"Miss?"

I look over and find the security guard watching me from the mouth of the foyer, his lips pursed.

He has a radio pressed to his ear and static issues from it. "My manager is pulling the camera footage now. Should we call the police?"

"No." God, I don't know why that word leaves my mouth. Or why my gaze won't leave the box. A foolish thought crosses my mind before I can quash it. How might Damien's gift differ from Simon's?

There's no mistaking who delivered this parcel for me. I smell him, tainting the air. Cologne. Mocking smugness.

I know as surely as I know my own name that he's overseeing this very moment. Waiting.

"I...I overreacted," I say, my voice rasping. "This came from a friend. You can go."

"Are you sure?" The security guard looks torn between the floral massacre and his crackling radio. "If you want to file a police report, it should be done as soon as—"

"I'm fine." I force a grin to prove it and nod toward the door. "Thank you. I'll contact the manager if I need anything else."

The moment the door closes after him, my posture deflates. Damn Damien. I almost wish he'd sent me something truly awful to put Simon to shame. Something I could march down to the police station or leak to the tabloids—possibly turning part of the vicious tide against Heyworth Thorne. *Something* to counter the sickly-sweet perfume of dying roses and prove once and for all that this gesture is a threat.

Or I could leave. Daddy wouldn't question too much if I returned home now with my tail between my legs. He'd prefer having me underfoot, always protected.

I'm still torn between the two possibilities when I finally cradle the present in my hands. It's lighter than expected. I undo the bow and strip the wrapping paper to reveal a wooden box with silver fixtures. After making sure no brooding madman is lurking in the shadows, I sit and lift the lid.

Inside, on a bed of red silk, rests a small sketch reinforced on a wooden base. I hate the gasp drawn from my throat when I recognize the woman staring up at me. At first glance, it's a chilling rendition: someone with features similar to my own, frozen in a mask of terror. A second glance, however, reveals something far worse.

The artist was skilled enough to depict everything down to the moisture glistening on her lips. The sweat slicking her skin. Her wide eyes and her bare chest heaving with bated breath. How her exposed throat almost demands raking teeth and violence. Destruction. *Lust.*

Poor woman, whoever she is. Damien violated her in charcoal and ivory.

In disgust, I flip the damned thing over and set it aside. Only to reach for it again and observe every line more closely.

I'm not sure how much time has passed when I finally notice the folded slip of paper lying in the box beneath where the sketch was. The message scribbled on it reads more like a command than a contrite request: *I assume this apology suffices. My studio. Tonight.*

A sound tears from my throat, startling me. Laughter? It's been so damn long since I've heard the real thing. No polite, restrained *hahaha*. I'm doubled over, clutching at my stomach as uncontrollable giggling reduces me to a quivering mess with streaming, watery eyes.

When I regain my composure, I rip up his stupid note and sprinkle its remains over the carpet of petals. Then I enter my bedroom, intending to pack. Return to Daddy. Damn Damien to Hell.

But the bastard didn't content himself with violating just one room of my suite. His scent conveys a haunting warning before I notice the lit lamp on my nightstand.

Someone left an object resting against its metallic base. Small. Black. Shaped like an earpiece.

That son of a bitch. Judging from the faint layer of dust on the device, it's been hidden, out of sight, for a while. Months, perhaps. Maybe even longer. I have no doubt that every bit of data and moment of vulnerability collected was used to create the profile of this vain, boring, materialistic woman he claims I am.

Tears prickle behind my eyes, and I choke down a desperate gulp of air. *Breathe.* He won't win tonight—I can't let him win. Without thinking through the consequences, I snatch up the device and bring it to my mouth.

"Enjoying the show?" I croak into it, hating how broken I sound. Fuck Damien. In fact… "You asked me if I was a virgin? Why? Is that how you get off? Manipulating women into bed? Does your blind-man act not earn enough pity on its own?"

Low blow, Thorne. I've never spoken to anyone like this before. Anyone. A thrill runs down my spine, feeding my resolve. Excitement, rather than shame.

"Sadly for you, I'd rather have sex with my doorman. Someone who doesn't need to paralyze his women to feel in control."

I break off, panting. For all intents and purposes, I'm shouting to myself. As far as I know, he could have severed this line. But no. A psychopath would never cut off communication with his victim first. He's listening, and I intend to give him a damn good show.

"Frankly, I'm disappointed, Mr. Villa." I creep toward my bed and mount the edge of the mattress. Unease flickers through my belly, but I ignore it. I've played by the rules of politeness for so damn long. He's pushed me to the brink.

"I thought you'd be better with your hands. Should I give you a demonstration, you sick bastard?" I turn, lying back on the mattress. My fingers flutter hesitantly before roving down my hip and finding the clasp of my jeans. "Listen and learn, Mr. Villa. You wanted something interesting to spy on, didn't you? Well, here's a sample of what you'll never hear in person."

I flick the bug aside without bothering to see where it lands. Somewhere close. Then I eye the ceiling and focus on...

I don't know. My hand seems to move on its own. It slides between my skin and the fabric of my underwear, finding the spot he assaulted that night. Damn it. The flesh feels different. Stimulated. Slightly sore. Because he's a bumbling, sloppy idiot—not because of the effects of the drug, rendering my body immobile against him.

It has no trouble at all reacting to me. One stroke of my finger along my entrance and I suck in a breath. I rarely have time for self-indulgence. Simon was always watching. Maybe he still is. I swallow hard and start to pull my hand away. But my finger crooks as if it has a mind of its own, stroking again. Faster. Harder.

Another, softer sound tears from my lips. A gasp. *There.* That's enough. Damien doesn't deserve any more of my debasement to entertain him. But even the thought of his name makes my chest tighten. It takes more effort to force air into my lungs. Because I hate him. Not because my traitorous body remembers what it felt like. His breath on my ear. His voice, hoarse and constrained—unsteady for once. *Are you a virgin?*

Why the hell did he care?

More importantly, why the hell can't I stop hearing him ask me that damn question?

Virginity. Virgin. Virginal. My hips arch against the bed. My touch becomes bolder, every finger desperate to recreate the friction he had. Almost. Almost… *Yes.* Sparks prickle as my finger flicks. I drive my teeth into my lower lip to smother the sound crawling up my throat. A groan rips from me, loud despite the attempt. He'll hear that and there's no taking it back.

Good. He can mock me all he wants. Sell the tape to the tabloids, even. But that will never erase the fact that he's listening. Right now, the artist is forced to bear my own form of art.

I stop thinking and let my body take what it wants. Rapid strokes. Deliberate motions. More. More. More.

But I don't feel the fire until my brain follows suit, displaying images without permission. Thick, soft fingers. A masculine voice reverberating through my skin. His taste on my tongue.

Hate must be the world's best aphrodisiac. My skin burns, overheated. Every breath doesn't feel sufficient. My eyes squeeze shut. Fingers curl.

There.

I only have the sense of mind to roll onto my stomach and smother whatever sounds I make into my duvet before everything inside me catches fire. Fuck Damien. I hate him. I swear I can hear him goading me on without an ounce of shame. *Don't tell me what you see, Ms. Thorne. Tell me what you feel.*

Empty. And stupid. And…lonely.

Boneless, I lie flat on my bed as my final cries echo back at me. The silken material of my duvet did a poor job of muffling them. Every word is clear. Make that a name ringing out as I pant and remove my hand from between my legs.

I give myself only a second to recover. Then I roll from the bed and hunt for the bug. I carry the damn thing into the bathroom, held between two fingers like a dirty piece of underwear. Damien's voyeuristic show ends with a splash as I drop the device into the toilet and flush it. After watching it disappear, I climb into the shower and scrub myself clean for the second time today.

Dripping wet, I crawl into bed without bothering to towel off. Before closing my eyes, I turn on every single lamp I own, flooding the entire suite with light.

And only now can I find some semblance of sleep.

Fitful, nightmare-ridden sleep, haunted by a man more terrifying than Simon.

Simon forced me to play his games.

I never initiated a round on my own.

FIFTEEN

Three days. That's how long I last alone, locked inside my suite without even work to distract me. Each one ends with me having to field a phone call from Daddy. Odd. Before, his customary checkups came weekly, disguised behind the pretense of casual conversation.

Tonight, he's far blunter. "I don't want you going out alone without calling for an escort."

I can tell from the background noise that he has the news on. A crisp-sounding reporter drones on about the latest headlines, but they're too faint to make out. I take a stab in the dark and guess. The Borgetta case.

"What happened?" I ask. Yesterday, he questioned me about my habits. Why wasn't I at work? Who knew that I had a detail following me? Why had I taken almost a minute to answer my phone?

"Nothing," he says too quickly. "They're calling for a storm tonight, so I just think you should stay in. I have to go. Have a wonderful evening, darling."

A wonderful evening. I'd laugh if the current state of my day weren't so pathetic. Without a television to use as a distraction, I lugged my old laptop from the recesses of my storage closet and spent the past twelve hours attempting to do work on the ancient dinosaur. For all I know, Damien bugged it as well. Just in case, I type FUCK YOU into a blank document, hoping whatever spying software he uses allows him to catch it. As my computer sluggishly attaches my finished files to my email, I open the browser and find myself hovering the mouse over the search bar.

The first news site I venture onto reveals an inkling of why Daddy's so on edge—and not just because of Damien. A witness in the Borgetta case was reported missing by his family and found dead hours later. No leads.

Not only that, but the article links to one with a headline that catches my notice: **The Curious Case of the Villa Family—and Their Money.**

According to the author, Damien immigrated to the US in his late teens with two younger brothers, Mateo and Mathias. Twenty years later, he's amassed a small fortune, but the circumstances surrounding his finances remain murky at best, and rumors of crime have dodged the family for decades—the worst of which was solidified when his youngest brother Mathias was convicted of Emily Borgetta's murder.

And my father was the judge who all but sentenced him to death.

I shouldn't pry anymore. Besides, Daddy told me all I needed to know of Damien. The key takeaway being: *madman*. I exit the browser only to find myself on the same page seconds later.

My, my. The topic of Damien certainly triggers an avalanche of search results. Thousands, actually. Dominating the top of the list are articles headlining his art and alter ego Sampson. Apparently, he doesn't go out of his way to hide that part of himself.

Most of the articles read as though they were written by sycophants who've never met the man in person, so different from the few cynical pieces regarding his family. *Artist captures the morbid honesty with dangerous charm.* That earns a snort from me. I've found more charm in a cactus than I could ever find in Damien.

Regardless, I keep clicking, determined to hunt down anything sordid. Bingo. He was at the center of a scandal once, which nearly tanked his investment business and dragged his name through the mud: the Borgetta murder.

Despite the fallout, he put the bulk of his fortune into his brother's defense fund as recently as this year. Each appeal brought new disturbing faces to light: potential evidence tampering, rumors of corruption in the prosecutor's office, and racial bias. In fact, the overturned conviction came almost entirely from Damien's dedication.

But it wasn't enough to save Mathias.

No wonder he hates my father.

I close my laptop and eye the view from my window while digesting the new information. So Daddy may have blurred a few of the facts. Why? I sigh rather than come up with an answer.

Gradually, darkness falls across the horizon, but I can't muster the strength to turn my lights on just yet. It's easier to face myself in the dark. How disgusting am I?

Not enough, apparently. Three days later and Damien has yet to respond to my parting gift. Not that he should. Screw him.

But that's the punchline, isn't it, a part of me taunts. *You want to.*

I don't. Despite everything, I barely even thought of him. During the day...

At night, my fingers took on a life of their own as my brain played a distorted slideshow of the night he drugged me. Over. And over. And over. Like a waking nightmare. One that left me gasping, and writhing, and flushing with a mixture of shame and guilt.

Fuck Damien. I almost want him to show up unannounced. It would give me a chance to play my final card. To see the look on his face when I call my father—

Speak of the devil.

There's someone at my door. The handle jiggles, sounding impossibly loud in the silence. I swallow hard and slip from the couch while flicking through possible culprits. It could be a security guard or one of the men Daddy put on my detail finally deigning to show his face.

Or…

Someone determined to get in *without* announcing their presence. Without knocking, they try the handle again. Roughly. After the stunt with the roses, I had the hotel change the locks. I can't shake the feeling that my visitor is caught off guard by that fact. They try the handle again. Again.

Only now am I aware of how late it is, past the hour when I'd usually be asleep. The perfect time for someone to slip in unannounced. Simon?

Air leaves my lungs in a rush. Before I can fully process my plan of action, I'm bounding into my bedroom on the tips of my toes. My phone is on my nightstand and I grab it, scrolling through my numbers. Daddy. The police. Someone. My trembling fingers can't seem to settle on a contact.

"Th-this isn't funny." I know he can't hear me. I threw the bug away.

Calling the police is a better course of action. I raise my phone to my mouth only to jump when a sound ricochets from the foyer. *Bang!* A sterner thud. Not merely a test of my handle, but a deliberate tug on it.

"If this is your idea of a joke…" I swallow the thought as my footsteps back me toward my closet. I'm a child again, drawn to obvious hiding places.

Hide. Run. Don't breathe.

The police never believed me then. They rarely do now. Good monsters know how to hide in the dark. How to master it.

"Stop," I tell the shadows as another thud reverberates from the hallway. "You win."

Bang!

Terror robs me of the ability to speak. My chest heaves as I stand against the closet door, clutching a heel I don't even remember grabbing from my floor. I brandish it in a shaking fist. Waiting... Waiting...

Finally, my tormentor grows bored and calls to me by name. "Open the door, Juliana."

God, it's like my body reboots at the sound of that accent. Then anger jolts me into action. I march into the foyer, and I don't bother to look through the peephole before throwing the door open. I can smell him.

Sure enough, he swallows the doorway, blocking the light from the hall. An enigma of black cotton and gray satin.

"You fucking bastard. How dare you—"

"Step aside!" He brusquely shoves me from his path as he says something else over his shoulder. Snarled words I don't understand. Spanish?

It's only when another man pushes past me that I realize who he's speaking to. Dressed in black and built like a bear, this newer man switches my lights on and prowls my suite with a hound-like intensity. I swear I hear him sniffing the air.

Denied my anger, I can only question, "What is this?"

His jaw clenched, Damien says nothing, leaving me to decipher what's happening on my own. They're searching for something. Someone. He's far too tense. Worried? If this is his way of apologizing, I'm not convinced.

After a few minutes, the brawny man reappears from down the hall. "*Claro*."

"Good," Damien replies. I'm not sure I've ever heard his voice so hard. His accent crackles like lightning over thunder. "Return to the lobby and survey the crowd. Report back if you see anything out of place. If not, take up a post on this floor. Somewhere discreet."

The man heads for the door. "*Sí*."

The moment he's gone, I whirl on the remaining intruder. My palms connect with his chest and I shove hard. He barely even flinches. Fine. I settle for slapping him instead. I've barely connected with his cheek before my wrist is captured in his grip.

"You're hysterical." He sounds as if he's trying to convince himself of that fact in order to maintain his composure. The last time I slapped him, he issued a warning. *I won't let it happen again.*

"*I'm* hysterical?" My voice echoes back to me. A stranger's. "You sick, fucking—"

"Whatever you experienced just now, I was not behind it." The certainty in his tone robs me of rage before I'm ready.

"Liar." I try hitting him again, but I miss. The world spins and I wind up clutching his forearm instead. Too tightly.

When he loosens his grip on my wrist, I expect him to shove me off. He finds my shoulder instead and loops his fingers around the sleeve of my T-shirt, keeping me upright.

"Trust me, Ms. Thorne. When I come for you, I won't have to break down your door."

I want him to be lying. Which makes no damn sense. He shouldn't be preferable to any other monster hunting me. Desperate to prove it, I latch onto the one thing his sudden arrival has made clear.

"How many bugs do you have hidden in my room?" My lips nearly graze his chest with every motion. He's too close. But he displays no intention to back away.

"Three. The one by your bed was the clearest, however."

"Well, I hope you enjoyed your final show," I tell him through gritted teeth.

He says nothing. *Oh?* I rake my gaze upward and find his expression…pinched? Unnaturally stiff jawline. Furrowed brow. He listened to my private show, all right.

And I should feel disgusted by that. Horribly violated.

Not…curious.

"Let go of me."

He does, but for some reason, my hand still grips him tightly.

"I want you to get the hell out—"

Darkness. Without warning, the lights shut off. A second later, lightning flashes.

And I'm miles away.

Are you afraid of the dark, Juliana? Think they'll find you soon?

Let's play another game.

"What's wrong?"

That voice was too deep. Not Simon. I blink, panting as I interpret my surroundings. Dark…but warm. No trees. I'm in my apartment again, but the man with me now shouldn't sound so damn concerned. And I shouldn't be clinging to him like a frightened child. I make a concerted effort to loosen my grip, but his hand remains on my shoulder, imparting just enough pressure to steady me.

"Power's out." I intend to sound unaffected. Not breathless. Blackouts were always the worst trigger. Sudden. Unexpected. After a summer of violent storms, Daddy had to buy a backup generator just to keep me—

"The outage must be a result of the storm," Damien replies smoothly. "There is a generator."

As if the building heeds his request, the power whirls back to life. My collection of lights would usually inspire relief. Not alarm. Apart from a voyeuristic asshole listening in, no one ever sees me like this. Panting. Eyes watering. Shaking.

"You should leave now," I croak, my obligatory rebuff. I don't sense any indication from him that he intends to. Yet, anyway.

Apparently, Damien has something he wants to say. I decide to beat him to the punch.

"Is that how you spy on me?" I'm eyeing the device attached to his left ear, barely noticeable against his dark hair. Only after a second do I realize he can't interpret the gesture. "With what's in your ear?"

He boldly fingers the device and lifts his shoulders in the semblance of a shrug. "I have a direct feed at another location." Smart man for not saying where. "This helps to supplement what I prefer to call oppositional research."

"Bullshit." Something about how he said "direct feed" makes me swallow hard. "You mean you have a dedicated room where you go to *spy* on me?"

The boring life of Juliana Thorne in HD surround sound, perhaps? Who's the dull one now?

"It's only recently that I've taken to keeping a more... consistent vigilance," he admits.

Consistent. My lungs promptly deflate of air. "Oh?" I wonder innocently, aware of how a muscle in his arm jerks beneath my touch. "How recently? As recently as three days ago?" I should leave it at that, but my lips won't stop moving. "When I gave you a taste of what you'll never, ever have?"

Bingo. He can't hide how his throat lurches, but an answering flutter in my chest alarms me far more. I flex my palm, intending to push away from him.

"Well, now that you mention it…" His fingers seize my chin, tilting it. At the same time, he lowers his face, bringing his mouth near my ear as if he memorized the distance. Close enough for his breath to fan my earlobe with every grated word. "It *was* as recently as three days ago," he concedes, "when you fingered yourself to the tune of my name. Or pretended to, perhaps…"

My cheeks flame. No one makes everyday words sound as vulgar as he does. *Fingered*. My own twitch against him. The last part of that statement, however, has my mouth contorting into a frown.

"Pretended?"

He can't see what I'm doing—I know that. Regardless, his nostrils flare anyway as if seeking every trace of the fingertips I parade beneath his nose.

"I definitely wasn't pretending." Only belatedly do I realize that statement could encompass everything. *To the tune of my name*. "About the f-fingering part."

"Oh?"

I shouldn't be able to track that shadow that falls across his features, even with the blindfold. He's dangerously easy to read in this moment. Tense. Waiting for something. A cue to leave, I think. And, God, I should give it to him. Get the hell out—but he's the one who started this game, and I can't resist taking one final cheap shot.

"Oh *yes*."

He tenses even before I hover my thumb over his lips. They're surprisingly pink. Soft. The slightest pressure is all it takes to make an indentation—and have him sharply inhale.

"If only you knew." I draw my hand away, fully intending to kick him out. I don't expect him to cup my face in retaliation, his thumb expertly finding my own mouth. I inhale raggedly, waiting.

He should leave it at that: a sleazy tit-for-tat. He shouldn't lean closer. I'm rendered motionless even though I have plenty of warning to turn my face. Run. Move. Something.

His mouth finds mine easily, separated only by the width of his thumb. "Oh, I would like to know," he breathes against my parted lips. "I'd *very much* like to know why you panted my name."

He sounds angry. Insulted. Intrigued.

Enough. I shove against him. At the same time, he lowers his hand and covers the distance between us.

Preemptively, I call his bluff. "You wouldn't dare—"

Our lips meet. Stiffen. Deepen their contact.

It's not a kiss. Even as his tongue swipes my mouth open and invades without warning. It's a battle of wits.

And I'm woefully unmatched.

He shouldn't taste sweet. Like cognac mixed with something fruity. Poisonous fruit. He rams his flavor into me like he's forcing me to swallow every illicit drop. He shouldn't feel so damn soft. My body shouldn't catch fire.

I shouldn't extend this.

He slides his hand around to the back of my throat, holding me captive as he steps in closer, using his height advantage as a weapon to knock me off-balance. My hands fly to his shoulders, clutching at the fabric of his suit jacket. Another searing taste of him unnerves me, deeper than the first. Another.

"S-stop." I break away and find myself stumbling in the direction of my room.

He follows me, eerily steady.

"Get out," I snap.

"Is that what you really want?"

Yes. My tongue struggles to push the word out as thunder rumbles ominously.

Days ago, I could face the threat of a simple storm alone without pacing before the row of windows in my living room or anxiously watching the clouds approach. I'd dread the thunder, but wine was my only defense—I had nothing to compare the loneliness to.

Now, when the first few drops of rain speckle the glass, there's no bottle within reach. Lightning flickers closer with every strike, heralding the terror of my past.

The woods.

Leslie.

His voice twisted its way through my skull.

Simon says...

"Juliana."

I whirl around, heart in my throat. "What?"

"You're afraid." He cocks his head, drawing attention to my current state. How I stand. How I breathe. How my gait wavers with every step I take over the carpet. "You're uneasy..." His posture stiffens and I imagine him listening for intruders in the shadows. When his search turns up nothing, he frowns. "Tell me why."

My teeth skewer my lower lip, trapping a frustrated hiss. I'm tearing my fingers through my hair like a madwoman. When lightning strikes, I jump.

"Fine." Teeth gritted, I turn from the window and find him seated, his posture erect. "Storms tend to usher bad men into my life." What I intend to be a cruel jab falls flat. I'm the one who winds up flinching.

"Bad men." He parrots the phrase emotionlessly. "Explain."

I force out a breath and turn on my heel. I'm treading the same path he was earlier. A ruthless trek from one corner of my living room to the other. My bare toes tingle as if sensing the steps he took, large and purposeful. *Ugh.* I shake my head to clear the thought. No use. The tingle spreads up my legs and I'm walking faster.

"I know you dug into my past," I say over my shoulder. "Don't pretend like you don't know."

"I'm aware of what happened to you as a child," he admits, phrasing the words with subtle care. "You were attacked in the woods by an unknown assailant. Your young friend was killed in front of you and you weren't found until over forty-eight hours later, on the verge of death. The murderer was never caught and some insensitive reporters sensationally suspected that you, an eight-year-old girl, may have been the culprit all along. Jealousy, they claimed."

I stare from the window, seeking refuge in the howling storm. I don't know why his knowledge shocks me so much. Of course he's done his research. Still. When most people discover my past, out come the kid gloves and coddling. Few would dare confront me about it in clinical, stark terms.

Fewer care to listen.

"I am aware of the published accounts, anyway," he adds. "I assume thunderstorms make you relive it."

I swallow hard. "Yes." God, I sound so damn pathetic. *He* does this to me. "It stormed that night…"

"When it happened?"

Forest. Cold. The memories threaten to unfold, but I bite them back. "How did you know someone was breaking in?"

"Intuition."

My eyes widen. "Are you magic in addition to blind—"

"You're stalling," he interjects. "What is it about the storms that makes you so afraid?"

My eyebrows furrow. "Desperate for a new emotion to paint, Mr. Villa?"

"No."

I shrug off the genuine curiosity in his tone. "They—" Lightning flickers across the horizon, and I lick my lips with a nervous flit of my tongue. "They make me feel...alone."

Alone.

Trapped.

Helpless.

Hopeless.

Lost.

"It was storming when you went missing," he deduces.

"Yes." Lightning flashes again and my apartment fades.

Gnarled trees loomed overhead, obscuring an indigo sky. Simon was watching. Hunting. Prowling.

Come out, come out, Juliana.

Cologne. My nostrils flare, chasing that scent, even as terror knots in my stomach. The more I breathe him in, the faster the forest recedes. Thunder bellows, rattling the walls, but I'm still here.

"When we went missing—when *I* went missing…my parents were too high and too drunk to notice for two damn days. I was hiding in a ditch in a hillside and I didn't move for so long my legs had grown numb. I couldn't even walk. A jogger found me, but they thought I was—" I break off, frowning, before I realize why.

Three-and-a-half whole sentences without interruption or a kind voice urging me to state how I "feel." A world record. He doesn't even press for the juicy details. What did he do to you? What did you see? Was he even real?

I almost wish he would. Or that I was brave enough to seek out a bottle of wine instead of him. Even alcohol can't loosen my tongue this much.

"Do you know what that's like? Hearing the world rage around you, bellowing and howling and knowing you're all alone. Your name isn't the one being shouted. No one can hear you screaming…"

I've said too much. My face feels strange. I reach up and find that my cheeks are wet.

"Is that when you received the scars on your hip?"

I glance at him sharply. He must have read my file. I can imagine how the crisp report described it: *Juliana, age eight, found with a seven-inch laceration on left thigh.* Has he known the answer all along and merely feigned his confusion before? Looking at him, I can't tell. He's fully focused on me, his head inclined, listening. Just listening.

"Y-yes." My fingers drift to my hip, tracing the old scar over the fabric of my pajama pants.

"And, afterward, you were adopted by Heyworth Thorne."

It's like he's feeding me lines from a fairytale I know by heart, skeptical but patient.

"Yes." I return to my view of the city and flatten my palms against the glass, framing the world outstretched below me. "You may think he's a racist, or incompetent, or whatever, but he saved my life. He saved me. I used to dream of what it would be like to live outside of the trailer park, you know? Never in a million years could I envision a place like this. A life like this."

"Did you know what he did before becoming a judge?"

"A defense attorney," I say. "It's why he accepted the appointment to the bench in the first place. He was tired of defending criminals. He wanted to put them away."

"And he told you this?" Damien wonders. I don't like his tone; it's too damn soft. "Interesting."

I sigh in lieu of dissecting his motives and watch my breath fog the glass. The silvery cloud obscures a nearby building, transforming it into a mass of yellow dots and inky darkness.

"Even now, I hate the rain," I murmur, the icing on my sordid little tale. "I really do."

"I've always enjoyed it," the man behind me confesses. He sounds too casual. As if sitting on my couch, discussing the weather is the most natural act in the world. As if this—us—is natural. "I used to enjoy watching the sky light up and feeling the moisture on my skin."

His use of past tense sticks out. I glance at him again, focusing on the blindfold. "And now?"

"I enjoy listening to it." His lips twitch into something not quite a smile, but not a frown, either. Wistful. "Someone told me once that every lash of thunder and drop of rain plays like music. A unique song only heard in that exact moment. Fleeting and never to be experienced by anyone again."

"That's quite a deep musing coming from a psychopath," I blurt. Surprisingly, he doesn't bite back. "Are you a musician as well?"

"No." He shakes his head. "Without my sight, I will never see a finished piece of my artwork. But, as you are aware, my hearing is quite intact. Not a second would go by without my hearing the flaws in any piece I created. Therefore, I'd create nothing."

So, he's a perfectionist *and* an accomplished stalker.

"Do you miss it? Seeing."

"No," he says without an ounce of hesitation. "I don't."

"Because you can hear just fine," I say pointedly. "In fact…"

I barge through my bedroom door and switch the light on. Three days have reduced my bed to a crumpled mass of sheets. My closet door is partially open with clothes thrown haphazardly on the floor of it. I look back and find Damien paused near the threshold, frowning as his foot warily taps my discarded heel.

Without thinking, I cross to him and kick the shoe from his path. Why? I have no damn idea.

"Where?" I demand, glancing around the room. "Where are the rest of your little toys?"

If I were a psychopath, where would I hide my secret listening devices? The drapes? Behind the potted plant in the corner? I make a show of loudly checking both places but come up short.

"Where?" I demand while marching toward him. "Maybe I'll even let you keep one. Poor man. I'd hate to deny you of your sole entertainment—"

"Ah, but I don't want to hear a recording of you moaning, Ms. Thorne."

My breath catches. He sounds too damn…heated. "Oh?" I croak. "Fine, then. Tell me where the other bugs are."

"No." He easily swats away the request and takes a step closer, homing in on my position. "But I'd much rather hear you moan in person."

I blink. *Breathe*. He's taunting me. "As if."

He takes another step and I'm frozen in place. Deliberately, he reaches for me, stroking his fingers along the side of my cheek. Then he cups the side of it. Deep down, I know that he's giving me all the time in the world to run. I don't. Not even when his lips claim mine once again.

I shiver as he tugs me forward. His tongue rims my mouth, a teasing request for entrance.

"S-stop," I croak without pulling away. I inhale his laugh directly.

"Do you really want me to?"

Yes. I want him to stop. But like a true madman, he doesn't give me the chance to demand it. His fingers trace my throat in a fiery caress, traveling down to my collar. Lower…lower still. My nipples sharpen in tense anticipation as he skims the cotton of my shirt. Pressing hard enough to sense but nowhere near hard enough to really feel. My mind plays a devious game of remembering how he felt after he'd drugged me. Raw heat over paralyzed muscles. I'm anything but frozen now.

My chest flutters. My toes sink into the carpet beneath them, desperate for leverage.

"You should leave, Mr. Villa," I breathe, hating how fragile my voice sounds in comparison to the muted storm raging outside.

He doesn't.

He steps forward, jarring my precarious balance. I assume he miscalculated my position for once—but no. He moves again, deliberately ramming his chest into mine, hard enough to jar back. Back. Back. My knees strike the base of my bed. Another firm nudge from him urges me onto it.

I stare up at him, panting. No matter how hard I try, I can't find enough air to command him to stop. And he knows too much—from the layout of my room, apparently, down to just how my body would fall when shoved onto my bed from this position. One of his hands captures my upper thigh and nothing in the world could prepare me for the cruel mixture of sensations jolting through my body. Fire. Ice. Slowly, his other hand finds my opposite thigh. He tugs, and my legs part, opening enough space for him to step in between.

"I suggest," he starts, his voice alarmingly thick. Guttural. "I suggest you…assist me, here. I'd rather not crush you."

I shudder at the word. *Crush*. And also what I know he left out. *Yet*.

When he nudges my hip, I'm reminded of his request. Assist him.

"To do what?" I've never heard this quality to my voice before. Husky. Like Sharla from accounting whenever Dave from research walks by her desk. Funny. I always thought Dave wasn't her type—but now I know.

Now, I know what it feels like to lie to yourself. It's hell. It's heroin.

In a breathtaking display of balance, he braces one knee against the mattress. I have to bite my lower lip as he uses my own thigh for reference to know where to place his limb, grinding against my flesh.

My hands fly out, finding his hips. An appreciative sound catches in my throat; the man is pure muscle. Coiled ridges of it flex beneath my touch as he braces one hand beside my hip. The other lands near my head, fisting in the sheets, and he's above me. My breaths fan his throat, disrupting the strands of hair framing his face.

"What are you doing?" I ask once I remember how to speak.

"Negotiating."

Thunder rumbles. Our lips meet again. Teeth. Biting. Tasting. Grinding—

Through the thin fabric of my pajamas, I feel the unmissable rasp of tailored fabric, heat, and…sin. I break away with a gasp. "Get…out—"

"The sheets."

From the corner of my eye, I see him raise a handful in his clenched fist. His nostrils flare inches from the fabric. His expression hardens.

"You didn't wash the sheets." His knuckles whiten, ivory over black silk. Shamelessly, he brings his fist to his nose again and inhales more deeply. A muscle in his jaw jumps, and I feel his chest expand, nearing mine.

He looks tenser than I've seen him. Poor Damien. My toes curl at the thought of just what he's seeking from my bedsheets. Or why he can't seem to let go of his fistful.

"We will make an exchange," he proposes, his voice composed once again, deep and suave. My inner thighs quiver as his lips part and a thick, red tongue traces the bottom one. "I'll give you the location of the remaining devices…"

"Good," I croak even as alarm bells go off inside my mind. This feels far too simple.

"And you…" His fingers find my lips as though magnetized to them. A newer scent blends in with his usual mix of aromas, and I almost miss his next words. "For every location, you give me something."

"Like what?" I muster up the courage to ask.

"A reward." His thumb grazes that dangerous sliver of space between my lips, imparting a million disturbing insinuations. "Something I can't capture with a mere recording."

"Y-you recorded me?" An image pops into my head of him locked in one of his cavernous rooms, replaying those sick, twisted tapes over and over again. "Why?"

From this angle, I have a perfect view of his twitching throat. Hard swallow after hard swallow. He doesn't say.

"And if I refuse?" I wonder as if that's really in question. I am going to. I will. "What? You'll sell your little recordings to the tabloids, hmm?"

"No." His upper lip curls back from his teeth at the mere suggestion. "I don't sell from my private collection."

Instantly, the heat in my belly cools. "Just how many recordings of women do you hoard?" I press my palm against his chest to push him off. "Goodnight, Mr. Villa—"

He shifts his weight to block my path. Trapped. His mouth grazes my ear from this angle and I feel the jolt down to my toes. Too damn close for comfort.

"What is your price?"

"I don't have one." I apply more pressure to his chest, but the bastard doesn't budge.

"Oh?" His voice deepens, heightening his accent. "I'll tell you the location of one of the devices in exchange for…a taste of what I'll never have." One shift of his weight and he has me pinned. Helpless. Limp. Breathless.

"What are you—"

Black. Darkness. Thunder.

Every light cuts off, plunging my room in shadow.

And I'm in the forest. Lost. Trapped.

"Let's play a game," he murmured, pointing from me to Leslie with the tip of a knife. *"Eeny, Meeny, Miny, Moe or rock-paper-scissors..."*

"Juliana."

The rough voice doesn't belong, combating Simon's slithering drawl. I cling to it, clawing my way to reality bit by bit. I see darkness. No forest. Lightning. A flash of my room. A shadow, reaching for me.

"Focus on my voice," someone snarls.

Oh no. There's vomit on my tongue. On the bed. I feel it running down my chin, hot like blood. Someone tries their best to wipe it away, utilizing a handkerchief.

"L-let me go!" I swat at his arm, but this time, he backs away.

It's unfair how easily he maneuvers, even in the dark. My eyes blink rapidly as I adjust to the loss of his heat. Too cold. Shivering. My fingers fan out, searching until they brush silk and curl around a fistful without permission.

"I'm here."

God, he's the last person in the world I should hear uttering those words. The last man on Earth whose reassurance should ease my heartbeat.

The last man in the world to drag me from a nightmare.

"Get out," I croak.

He doesn't move and the minutes of the outage tick by, longer than the first. Too long.

"Let's play a game," he said. "Eeny, Meeny, Miny, Moe or rock-paper-scissors? What about you, little girl in the purple... Tell us what to play."

"Are you listening to me? I think I just insulted you, Ms. Thorne."

Huh? I blink. Still here, in my room. With Damien...

"I said," he says, infuriatingly calm, "that your bed is a travesty. *Sí*, no wonder you've been moaning every night."

Heat creeps into my cheeks. "B-bastard."

"I thought women like you lounged on silk?"

"Fuck you." The retort trickles out of me, more as a whisper than anything else. "Go away."

"I would," he says thickly. "If you let me go."

I stiffen, aware of my grip on him, but I can't seem to loosen it. Out of self-preservation, of course. If this is a stunt, I'll make sure his DNA is beneath my fingernails. I'll make sure the world knows that Damien entered my apartment and...

"Your heart is racing," he declares, sounding more concerned than taunting. "You're afraid—"

"Get out!" This time, I manage to shove him off just as a ripple of thunder reverberates through the walls.

"Pick," a cruel voice demanded. *"Who will live and who will die?"*

"Damn." The harsher, deeper baritone doesn't belong in my memory.

Blinking, I return to the present. I'm in my room. On my bed...

Someone's fingers are in my hair as more warm liquid drips from my mouth and down my chin.

"Get off," I croak, swiping at my lips. Panic melds in my blood, making everything too loud. Too sharp. Too hot.

"Breathe," someone urges against my ear. Their hands slip from my hair, following the curve of my spine. "Breathe."

My lungs obey him, sucking in air as the chilling reality sinks in. There's vomit on my shirt. I'm shaking and the past looms, waiting for another roll of thunder to overwhelm me again.

And Damien is here to witness every terrible second.

"Get out." I shift away from him and brace my feet on the floor, but he follows, his heat like a wall, keeping me upright.

"Close your eyes," he commands against the nape of my neck. "Now."

I do, and the darkness doesn't help ease the shame setting my cheeks on fire. "Lucky you," I rasp. "You have a wonderful story to sell to the tabloids—"

"Take off the shirt."

My blood goes cold and the reality of the situation descends at full force: I'm alone in my room with a stranger.

"W-what?"

"It's filthy." He sounds so calm. So logical. "You need to change."

But my closet is too terrifying a territory to venture into now.

"You're disgusting," I spit, even as I shrug the shirt over my head and toss it aside. "Only a pervert would get a woman naked at a moment like—"

"You can insult me," he counters, still so damn unshakeable, "if it helps distract you. I can make an exception this once."

An exception?

"Get out—"

"I can think of a better distraction than anger, however." The shift in his tone sends my pulse racing. Another roar of thunder echoes, but it sounds too distant now, no match for his low, dangerous rasp. "When you performed your little exhibition, where exactly did you touch yourself?"

I can't breathe, but this time, it's not because of terror.

"You disgust me," I hiss.

"Show me," he counters. "Or was it all an act?"

A shiver runs down my spine as he adjusts himself behind me. On either side of my hips, his hands appear outstretched, painted silver as lightning flashes.

"You want me to paint you," he reminds me, his breath hot on my skin. "You think you can bare every inch of yourself to me? You truly believe you're brave enough to face that woman? I think you're lying to yourself, Juliana." Thunder mingles with his words, sending a thrill through me. "I think you're damn good at lying—"

I grab his hand and place it against my thigh.

We both go rigid.

His fingers are too damn soft. Mine shake as awareness of the storm threatens to shatter even his twisted "distraction." I can taste the forest again. See it…

Just as the memory unfolds, Damien asks, "Was it here?"

I gasp.

His fingers travel without permission. I'm back firmly in the here and now, suffocating as the tip of a thumb nudges tender flesh.

"Or here?" He drifts higher, sweeping his touch up the ridge of my belly. "I doubt you're bold enough to go lower."

"I-I told you," I manage to reply in a rush. "You'll never have—"

"Or maybe here?" His other hand cups the opposite hip, applying just enough pressure to tease an ounce of fear from my frayed nerves.

For a second, I toy with the potential danger. He could rape me.

But he won't. A man like him wouldn't see the fun in that.

"You wouldn't dare," I tell him, confident of that fact. My eyes are closed again and reading him now is easier than ever. He's brutal, Damien. Never reckless. He wouldn't give me the satisfaction of ever claiming assault. "Men like you don't get their hands dirty."

"No?" he retorts in a low murmur. "If not to hurt you, then what might my motives be?"

He's distracting me, as much as it stings to admit that. His fingers are my only anchor against the past and Simon. Two monsters go to war on my psyche, but one wins out.

"It was lower," I admit, breathless. His fingers twitch, hesitant to move. "A place you will never, ever touch—"

"But I have touched you there," he points out, chuckling in a grated, tortured way. "In fact, I doubt many men have. So tight. Barely accepting of one finger."

There's awe in his tone. Smugness too.

"I can accept my fingers just fine," I snap.

"I can imagine."

I jump at the barely concealed dare. *So do it, then.*

My fingers tremble as they brush over the fabric of my pants. Every cell in my body warns me to run. But I don't. I find the drawstring instead, arching my hips to undo it.

And the atmosphere changes. His grip tightens, biting in deeper.

"It was here," I tell him, sliding a hand between my legs. He shouldn't be able to tell. I could be lying.

But he knows the second I make contact. His breathing changes. His posture tenses.

I've won the game.

But the rules have changed from here on out. It's not enough to accept his dare. The second I attempt to pull my hand back, his falls over my wrist, conveying a silent command through only a subtle bit of pressure.

Show me.

I squeeze my eyes shut as traitorous heat builds and spreads. My legs drift apart before I can help it. My hand slips lower. His becomes a vise.

And nothing else matters. Not the thunder biting through the silence. Not lightning. Not Simon.

I touch myself.

He listens, inhaling harshly against my earlobe, his touch tracking every shameful motion.

It's my previous show in HD surround sound.

And I don't care if he records this moment and sends the tape to the news.

He makes for a chilling barrier against the darkness as heat builds inside me. For a dangerous second, I imagine his hand drifting lower and pushing mine out of the way...

A gasp slips from my throat and wetness coats my fingers. Too much. Too real.

"You're close, aren't you?" His lips part near my jaw and my nerves rattle. With one quip, he could devastate me. Humiliate. "Let go," he demands instead, his voice like a spark over tinder.

I catch fire.

My eyes flutter shut as my back arches. I'm leaning against him. Into him, letting the heat drown out shame until all I can feel is an agonizing inferno.

"Should I paint you like this?" He sounds on the edge of a groan as I spasm against his chest.

At the back of my mind, I know I should be embarrassed. Horrified, even. Not writhing through every tortured second he extends his nearness.

"Coiled muscle, sweat-slick skin, panting," he murmurs into my ear, painting a picture with his fucking voice alone. "Hang it where your father might see? His beautiful girl... So broken. So shameless."

My face inflames at the thought and enough shame leeches into my dazed brain that I withdraw my hand. "Would you?"

A brush of his knuckles over my wrist doesn't give me a solid answer. "How many fingers was it?" he wonders, half taunting, half serious. "That you used that night—"

I force out a laugh. "Wouldn't you like to know?"

His own fingers flick my skin in tandem as if to convey silent guesses. One? Two? Five?

But he doesn't force me any further, dragging me right to the edge of some invisible boundary that I didn't even know was there.

He waits, letting me keep the fragile reins of control.

And only now do I realize that the rain has stopped.

The storm has passed.

SIXTEEN

*U*h-oh. The ominous thought tugs me awake and my brain sluggishly tries to decipher why. There are the usual suspects. Uh-oh, I'm late for work. Uh-oh, I'm having a horrendous flashback. Uh-oh, Daddy's pounding on my door, demanding I reassure him of how happy and healthy I am.

All of those would be preferable to the slow realization that someone else is in my bed. Someone large, their limbs skewing the surface of my mattress to one side. Someone who smells of sin and cognac, and inexplicably of roses.

Uh-oh.

I peel my eyes open to a view of my ceiling. Gray daylight streams across it, alluding to a final break in the storms. If only that peace could translate into my current reality.

Even his breathing resembles thunder. Low and unassuming until I finally notice it. With every additional note, I find myself tensing with the next unnerving rumble.

I turn in his likely direction, all the while desperately gathering up the nerve to do what must be done. Scream. Fight. Kick him the hell out.

Or stare.

He's a creature made of shadow who has an unholy affair with sunlight. No matter how faint, it paints detail into his skin, fleshing out what dimmer surroundings disguise. Like the subtle lines around his mouth that hint at his age. The faint gold in his skin. The blue-black tint to his hair, and the slight quirk in his jaw that betrays when he's awake.

"Good morning, Ms. Thorne."

"I could have you arrested for trespassing," I tell him, hoping I sound intimidating enough. Not exhausted. Uh-oh, uh-oh. There's a bitter taste on my tongue. Residue from a horrific flashback. I can only recall snippets. Good. I don't remember the gist. Just that...

I clung to someone. Someone who coached me through the nightmare, their voice a rugged anchor. Someone who held me through gasping sobs. Someone with an accent like hellfire.

"You vomited," he says. "Afterward, you removed the shirt."

The blunt warning precedes the moment I finally look down and realize the horrifying truth. It comes in the pair of gray panties I'm wearing—nothing else.

"Y-you stripped me." I instinctively cover my breasts with my hands.

"I'll avert my gaze if you'd like," Damien says dryly.

So the man has jokes. Apparently, my realizing that I slept mostly naked next to a psychopath amuses him.

Or not. His expression is tense. I can decipher the emotion conveyed on his face clearly, even with the blindfold obscuring most of it. Annoyance.

"Why…why did you stay?" My confusion confounds me almost as much as my lack of real anger does.

He's right. A foul stench taints the air, and my vomit-soaked shirt is on the floor, neatly folded. I have a vague image in my head ripping the soiled clothing off by myself.

And I huddled against him rather than move. Something I rectify now by lurching from the mattress and into my closet. I snatch the first garment I see from its hanger and pull it on: a black cocktail dress worth more than Sharla from accounting's weekly wages. And I just ruined it with vomit and tears.

To save face, I enter my room with my head held high as though I'm totally unaffected by the sight of Damien standing near my bed.

"I assume your father had good intentions when he hired your current security detail," he says, sounding oddly neutral. "However, I shall take the liberty of installing my own men from now on. I can assure you that you won't have a repeat of last night."

Did he mean the near break-in, his impromptu visit, or both? I shake my head to clear it. Neither matters.

"I suppose I should feel flattered," I admit. "Bodyguards installed by a criminal. I'm sure they excel at murder, and extortion, and whatever sordid talents men like you value."

He doesn't even wince. "When necessary."

God, he actually sounds serious. A concerned Damien is the last thing I need.

"Why should you care?" I demand, placing my hands on my hips. "You hate my father. I bet you loved seeing me terrified—"

"You're right. I despise your father, and you are the single most devastating weapon I can use against him. But I prefer to utilize you on my terms, as I see fit."

Can't blame the man for honesty. "Well, you certainly don't mince words," I quip.

"And you aren't foolish," he counters. "Accept my offer."

I should refuse. That would be the smart, logical thing to do. But smart and logical don't apply to seeking safety in the arms of a psychopath.

As if reading my mind, he adds, "I won't always be there to listen for your nightly performances, Ms. Thorne."

I puff up indignantly and bite back a sigh of relief. Anger is a weapon I need now more than ever—I won't acknowledge the fact he gave it to me.

"Do what you want, Mr. Villa." I make a show of marching into the living room. Loudly. My heavy footsteps barely drown out the slower, heavier ones in my wake. "Just so long as your offer doesn't include *you*."

"This one doesn't."

I look back and find him advancing from the hall.

"My next proposal, well... That will require some negotiation."

I don't take the bait right away. I nearly run to my coffee maker and fumble with the settings until something dark and steaming pours into a mug. Only after I've drained every last drop of liquid do I bite. "And what proposal would that be?"

"Dinner. With me. Tonight."

"Dinner." I hum thoughtfully and tap my chin. "Let me guess. You'll take me to an orgy this time—"

"Dinner," he insists. "A meal. You and I. Entirely business in nature. We would both be allowed to question each other, and both be required to answer. Honestly."

I frown and search through my cupboards for another pack of instant coffee. "Frankly, Mr. Villa, I have to wonder why you'd want to question me. I'm Juliana Thorne, and as you've said more than once, there isn't anything interesting about me."

"I'm sure there is plenty you would like to know about me," he counters as he starts for the door and opens it. "The next time you search for me online, remember that there are two Ls in my name. Enjoy the rest of your day, Ms. Thorne. Oh, and Julio will be your guard for this evening. He'll stay out of sight."

"Dinner…" I draw the word out, only mildly entertained by watching him linger. Oh, he doesn't want to. I could bounce pennies off the tension coiled in his shoulders. "I'm terribly busy, Mr. Villa."

He takes a step.

I raise my voice. "But…"

Again, he pauses. For a second. Two. The fact blows my mind. He's a man with a criminal empire to run, frozen at my doorstep in anticipation of whether or not I'll accept a dinner invitation. "If I can find the time, how should I reach you? Scream into my wallpaper?"

"Ah…" He chuckles darkly. "But as you yourself have said, I have more important matters to amuse myself with than the life of Juliana Thorne. Have a good day. *Adiós*."

He leaves, for real this time. I don't bother taunting him back.

I sip fresh coffee like the antidote to his poison only to find myself eyeing the very real toxic gift he left for me. I don't normally keep plants on principle. They require even the bare minimum attempts at nurturing—something that was never my forte. Still, I take a stab in the dark and assume this one needs water. Surprisingly, its delicate petals haven't started to wither. They cast the faintest aroma that itches my nostrils. It's deceptively sweet. Like roses, laced with sugary candy. You'd never know that one nibble could be deadly.

If there were a person as sweet and as innocent as oleander, Daddy wouldn't think twice before letting them off, despite what the evidence may say. They weren't menacing. Not like Damien or his brothers who alarmed and inspired unease on sight.

Therefore… I drag my finger across my neck and mouth another one of Daddy's chosen phrases, "Guilty as sin."

But what does that make me? Oleander, or snarling imposter weeds?

The question haunts me as my cell phone rings.

"Juliana," my father says from the other end. "I've made all of the arrangements for tomorrow. All you have to do is attend."

"T-tomorrow?"

"The press conference," he says, exasperated. "I'm having a dress sent over. It will be at ten sharp, and I'll have a car sent for you an hour before."

"Of course… See you then."

The looming prospect of media attention makes for the perfect foil to Damien's visit last night. I'm haunted by both as I strip my dress and shower, scrubbing vigorously to erase every trace of the blind psychopath. When I return to my room to tidy it, I groan and wring my hands in exasperation. Someone already has—attempted to, anyway. They straightened my sheets. Removed the soiled clothing from my floor and placed it in the hamper near my closet. They also presumably tripped over the heels I left scattered near the door.

I don't clean for him. Neither is he the reason why I strip my sheets and replace them with fresh ones. So maybe I rustle the sheets loudly enough for a speaker to pick up from some hidden location. According to his smug insinuation, he won't be listening. So he certainly won't hear the reluctant sigh that tears from my chest.

"Dinner," I blurt, hating how my voice echoes in the silence. "We do this on *my* terms. Nowhere public, but somewhere with plenty of exits in sight. If I feel cornered, I'm leaving. If I feel threatened, I'm leaving. I decide what we eat, and most importantly—I ask the first questions." I pause, belatedly realizing that he won't answer back. Feeling my cheeks flame, I soldier on. "Have a car waiting for me at seven. A minute later and I'm not going. Though I suppose I might as well not bother at all. You're far too busy to be listening."

There. Empowered, I shrug nonchalantly as if performing for a camera—though, who knows, maybe I am. Good. I hope the bastard has someone there to give him a very vivid description of my ass as I stoop for a pair of heels, grab my coat, and promptly escape my apartment.

I enter a hall and jump at the sight of a large man leaning against the wall at the other end. Only his vaguely familiar features keep my heart from pounding its way from my chest. He nods to me slowly in greeting. When I head to the elevator, he doesn't follow. Yet I can't shake this lingering suspicion that I'm never alone. Someone is watching me—and not quite as predatorily as Simon.

Speaking of which…

My old friend hasn't asserted his existence yet. I should feel relieved, but I don't. Just tense. It's not a matter of if he'll resurface.

It's when.

SEVENTEEN

*S*even rolls around and I'm still in my apartment, blissfully unhurried. After all, there's no point in waiting for a ride that will never show—or so I tell myself.

Following that logic, there was no reason to get dressed, either. No reason to wash and blow out my hair or paint my lips in the one shade I have other than red: a slightly lighter pink. There's certainly no reason to glare at my reflection and wrestle with the idea of changing for the umpteenth time.

In the end, I'm still scowling when I finally leave the bathroom and don my coat. I'll head down out of pure curiosity. Being stood up—in theory—will just give me more ammunition to use against Damien. At least I'll prove he was lying about the bugs.

Just for fun, I pause near the foyer and tilt my head toward the ceiling, scanning for little black devices. "I want pizza," I say. "The extra-cheese special from Georgianos. They know me there, and I'm the only one in the world who orders that special, so there will be a record of your address that my father can trace if I go missing."

It's a bald-faced lie. I haven't ordered from Georgianos in months—though he doesn't know that. Then again, the bastard did bug both my home and my office for an undetermined amount of time. In any case, I can take comfort in the fact Mr. Damien Villa has already expressed boredom from spying on me.

Though I still find one of his men in the hallway when I step out of my suite. Dressed in black, he greets me with a nod. Downstairs, I spot two similarly dressed men lurking amongst the crowd. They don't acknowledge me directly, but I sense them watching as I head for the main doors. Outside, a sleek vehicle is waiting for me. The driver stands beside the passenger's door and opens it as if on cue.

"Good evening, Ms. Thorne."

Damn Damien. So the bastard called my bluff after all. In the process, he gave himself away; he's been listening to my boring life in real time.

Gritting my teeth, I enter the car and try to ignore the alarm bells going off in my mind. This could be a trick. A rather elaborate one, admittedly. Any time during the day, Julio could have barged into my apartment and done whatever he wanted.

Perhaps Mr. Villa preferred to do the deed himself? Luckily for him, I'm being hand-delivered.

He isn't far. My destination turns out to be only blocks from my building, in the same upscale part of town: an even taller skyscraper formed of black glass and gold accents. It's a breathtaking bastion of wealth, but there's no clear indicator as to its purpose. Evil lair? Reclusive penthouse dwelling?

Inside, a plain lobby with granite floors and dark walls funnels any visitor to a gilded elevator.

"Take it to the roof," the driver instructs, having come inside with me.

He leaves, and I ride the elevator up alone, desperate to quell my staggered heartbeat. When the elevator doors finally part, I'm forced to acknowledge my first concession of the night: Damien followed my instructions perfectly.

The private roof, several stories above most surrounding buildings, certainly isn't within obvious public view. Score one. The low barrier keeping an occupant from plunging to their death could technically be viewed as an abundance of "exits." But only a sadist would interpret "I don't want to feel cornered" as a license to host their morbid soiree inside of a structure composed almost entirely of glass.

It dominates the center of the rooftop, illuminated with golden light. I blink several times before I dare put a name to it: a greenhouse.

A real one.

I can smell the flowers from here. Sweet. Fresh. An amalgam of color bolsters the different scents: spicy, delicate, aromatic. Too many to name. I'd stake my life on the assumption that roses are among them.

When I don't spot Damien lurking within the shadows, I warily approach the pair of glass doors serving as the greenhouse's entrance. They open easily, and I smother a sigh as a comfortable warmth replaces the frigid night air. My eyes blink to adjust, and for good reason.

It's like I left winter and entered spring—if mother nature happened to be a passive-aggressive perfectionist.

Countless plants are arranged neatly in black planters, spread out at meticulous intervals. There isn't so much as a wayward petal on the stone flooring, and I could walk the orderly paths…well, blindfolded. A vital feature, I'm willing to admit, given the limitations of the man sensing my approach from beside a selection of his signature flowers.

Red. White. Yellow. Pink. Roses in every hue imaginable sprout around him, a morbid rainbow, clashing with the black of his suit and matching blindfold. Here, Damien sticks out more than ever: a glaring stain on this otherwise paradise.

"I hope this is suitable to your terms," he says dryly.

"It's not a sex club, at least." I fight to keep awe from my tone. "I hope you don't think that bringing me here will make me let my guard down. I've never been that sort of woman."

The kind to fall for extravagant gestures such as a private dinner among a makeshift field of flowers. Then again, I've never been the sort of woman whom men made such gestures for on a regular basis.

"I'm not sure what you mean."

He has his head cocked, confused as he processes my words. Oh. I could kick myself. Obviously, he isn't aware of how this venue might appear to someone. Which makes it doubly infuriating that he brought me here. Why?

Could the choice be entirely personal rather than meant to intimidate? Maybe. He wants to confront me on familiar ground.

"Did you plant all these yourself?" A tendril of appreciation makes it harder to seethe. I'm wandering the nearest row before I can stop myself, reaching out a finger to brush a soft bloom—a dangerous act in the world of Damien. "I hope this isn't oleander?" I ask belatedly.

"Toxic shrubs are in the righthand alcove," he replies. "And I require assistance, but I care for what I can."

He sounds…hesitant. Each word is clipped. Defensive. The same way he sounds whenever I mention one of his paintings. He thinks I'm mocking him.

"It…it's beautiful." My body deflates with the admission and I keep wandering, brushing flowers as gently as I can. Just to make sure they're real and not plastic.

He follows me, keeping a cautious distance.

"I'm assuming this is where my 'toxic shrub' came from?" The righthand alcove. I find an area slightly set apart from the main display. Those boxes are silver, which gives the plants they hold a mysterious air.

"No. I know a supplier whom I trust, but I would never discard one of my plants." Judging from his tone, he could have substituted another word: *I would never murder one of my plants.*

Not for the first time, he displays obsessive protectiveness of his work. Even sending a thinly veiled threat to a target is seen by him as wasteful.

"And the roses?" I wonder. Unsurprisingly, his appear unmolested. I doubt my floor is good enough to be graced with Damien's hand-grown creations.

"Also purchased." He sounds closer.

Perhaps because I've stopped walking, riveted by a blossom unlike any I've ever seen. Ebony petals form a cup with a wash of light pink inside. I tentatively finger a petal; it's so soft, one touch feels liable to tear it.

"A black orchid," Damien explains. He must have the layout memorized, down to the location of each blossom. "Ironic, considering you don't seem to be wearing that color tonight..." His nostrils flare. Maybe the bastard really can sense color by smell.

For the first time since leaving my suite, I look down at my dress and lament forsaking my chosen color. I went to the boutique earlier today—one I've frequented for years. When I requested something in "a more colorful shade," the saleswoman looked as though I'd proposed ending world peace with a wave of my manicured hand. In a daze, she wandered into the back room and returned with this.

A blood-red number in the same shade as his massacred roses. The fabric feels too thin, a mixture of satin and lace. The neckline plunges a hairsbreadth too low, displaying nonexistent cleavage. All in all, it's a garment so unlike my usual style that I wouldn't recognize myself.

"Well?" I confidently appraise my opponent. No earpiece tonight—unless he hid it. No lackeys nearby to feed him all the right answers either.

Just me and him. A level playing field for once?

"What color am I now?" I extend my arms, offering myself up for his scrutiny. "Oh, Damien, all-knowing stalker of Juliana Thorne. Tell me how I look. Bonus points if you can describe it based on *smell*."

Mocking a blind person may be wrong in a different context, but I'm prepared to make an exception. Until he steps forward and inhales me deeply, without warning or permission.

"Oh, I can't be sure, Ms. Thorne, what with my *disability*…" He reaches for me, finding my shoulder. Two of his fingers tease the spaghetti strap of my dress and follow it down to the lacy neckline, heedless of the exposed flesh beneath.

He knows just how to unnerve me. Where to touch so I can't claim indecency. As well as the exact moment to pull his hand away and bring it to his mouth.

I expect him to rub his chin thoughtfully. Not run his thumb directly over his lower lip as if tasting scarlet on my skin.

"Why, Juliana, I have to say, you smell divine in *red*."

Bastard. "You cheated," I snarl, turning away from him. "What, did you have me followed to the boutique?"

"Come here." The command lacing his voice alone should give me the cue I need to leave.

He doesn't own me. He certainly can't order me to do his bidding. But perhaps that's the infuriating part? He isn't. No matter how many seconds tick past, he doesn't come after me. Doesn't reach for me. I don't even hear him breathing heavily to indicate anger. No, he merely proposed a dare. *Come here and learn the answer for yourself.*

I don't give him the satisfaction of responding. Instead, I turn on my heel and cross to him.

He captures my forearms from either side. A gasp escapes my throat, but before I can even think to fight, he loosens his grip and one of his hands drifts up to my chest.

"Your heart is racing," he explains, grazing a nail over the muscle in question. I feel it lurch, assaulted by his touch even through layers of skin and bone. "You're uncomfortable. Red is a bold color. You feel unsure wearing it. Though I did accuse you of being dull. It's only fitting that you would select the boldest hue in response."

He sounds so damn smug, as if he has me pegged down to the last cell and strand of hair. When I raise my hand, he predictably seizes my wrist.

"I wasn't going to slap you," I admit.

After a deliberate second, he lets me go and I bring my hand inches from his face, hating how my fingers shake. With effort, I calm them enough to trace the line of his jaw, shivering at how he clenches it against me. So damn suspicious.

"You think you know me, but I've already got you sussed," I tell him, fighting to keep my voice steady.

Touching him at all was a mistake. His heat isn't repulsive even in the humid greenhouse. His skin feels as soft as his hands, and the closer my fingers drift toward his mouth, the more I'm reminded of how his lips felt against mine. Swallowing hard, I step back and flatten both of my hands against my hips.

"You think I'm so predictable," I say, "but you're worse. You're infallible. So desperate for control you can't have one little thing go wrong. Can you?"

Alarm drips down my spine even before I follow through on my foolish impulse. I reach for an orchid and use both hands to snap a bud free. The violent crunch echoes like a gunshot and Damien looks…

Consuming.

He advances on me swiftly, capturing my chin in his grip. His nostrils flare with the aroma of his ruined flower. His shoulder tenses. I know he'll hit me. I'm ready for it. Maybe I want him to.

Violence would give me a reason to hate him more. Something to counter the image of the man who held me while I broke. The same man shamelessly haunting me, claiming to know me better than I do. I'd take any reason.

All he does is cruelly drag his thumb up to my mouth and apply enough pressure to force my lips apart. He steps in closer at the same time, allowing his breath to fan my throat in a teasing swipe.

Anger has a smell on him too, but I wouldn't dare attach it to a color. Maybe a phenomenon: *lightning*. Striking without warning and inflicting untold damage. Breathing is an ordeal. Sweat slicks my skin, affecting his grip. It tightens, tilting my head back farther, in the prime position for his mouth to claim mine if he wanted. Bite. Consume.

Suddenly, he lets me go and I cling to a nearby planter for balance, still holding my severed orchid.

"Put it on the table, *por favor*," he snaps to a man who I didn't even notice has entered the structure.

Wearing a suit and tie, he blends in with the other nameless men who I assumed work for Damien—minus the object he's carrying. I do a double take and wind up tightening my grip on the planter. The rich smell flooding my nostrils proves that the sight isn't a figment of my imagination: a large box of pizza fresh from Georgianos.

"Shall we?" Damien inclines his head. "I believe we've wasted enough time."

We have. Back to the task at hand, the only reason why I came here in the first place: for answers.

"Fine." I follow him down the aisle and into a small section cordoned off from the main greenhouse by a wall of glass.

The man with the pizza sets it onto a small table flanked by two strategically placed chairs.

"Dismissed," Damien says to him, and the man leaves without a word. Then my host tilts his head toward me. "Sit."

I eye the table warily. Pizza with a madman. Oddly enough, I've had worse dining companions. The governor's disgusting son who spit food while he ate. The lecherous old senator Daddy tried to woo for support.

Damien Villa isn't the least appealing, admittedly. So, I take the chair nearest to me while he claims the opposite one. Once seated, he gestures toward the box of pizza.

"As you requested."

He's not gloating for once. Something tells me that pizza wouldn't be on the menu if he had his way. Good. I drag the box toward me and flip the lid open. It smells even better than I remember, cooked exactly to my preference.

"How do I know it's not poisoned?" If so, it's too late; my fingers have already staked claim over a slice.

"It isn't," he says. "Though I'll admit that I've considered it."

I wrench my fingers from a strip of crust. "What? Why? Have I bored you to the point of murder?"

"Who said anything about killing you?" The grudging honesty in his tone is enough to help air trickle back into my lungs. For now. "No. I'm nowhere near finished with you yet. So eat."

"So…" I toy with a different slice. "Was your aim to paralyze me, then?"

His glowering posture makes me aware of how I'm sitting: legs crossed, my free hand knotted in a fist to hide how it trembles.

"That is a matter we will discuss at another time. For now, I've humored your requests, so get the remaining one out of the way and ask your questions." His tone reveals the threat he's holding back. *Then I'll ask mine.*

I find myself eyeing the corners of the room, desperate to stall this moment. There are so many damn things to ask. Looking at him, I settle on the most obvious. "Were you born blind?"

I already suspect the answer before he shakes his head. His drawings are far too detailed. Too raw. He must have some prior knowledge of the human body. Of women, and flowers, and lust-filled glances.

When he doesn't speak, I'm prepared to accuse him of breaking our agreement. Before my lips can even part, he reaches behind his head. One tug of his fingers and the blindfold falls away.

"I apologize in advance for your appetite."

Food quickly becomes the last thing on my mind. Faced with all of Damien, I can't breathe.

I knew he was handsome, even with so much of his face obscured. Taking him in fully, I'm forced to admit that the man is nothing short of beautiful. Strong nose. Elegantly arched eyebrows. Chiseled cheekbones. He's striking, despite the two vertical scars sealing his eyes shut. They're silvered. Old. At least one of my theories is thoroughly debunked: He can't see at all.

Horror robs me of any snarky response. I move my lips several times before I can croak out an actual word. "H-how?"

He bears the scrutiny for a few seconds longer before retying his blindfold with an ease that betrays years of practice. "I'll spare you the dramatics," he says simply. "One might say that I blinded myself."

I'm not sure if I gasp or say something intelligible. Whatever I do makes his jaw clench, and he's suddenly stone.

"I'll preemptively answer your next question. Why? I can assure you that you wouldn't understand the reason."

He's lying. No one could inflict wounds like that on their enemies, let alone themselves. I wouldn't wish that agony on anyone. Even Simon.

"H-how long?"

He frowns as if he's never stopped to tally up the years before. "Fifteen years," he says finally. "I... It happened when I was nineteen."

Which makes him only a few years older than I am. Odd. He seems so much older. A wizened man trapped inside the body of an exotically colored Adonis.

Curiosity keeps me questioning, even as the image of his scars lingers in my mind. "Where are you from?"

"A village in South America," he says, "in a region you've most likely never heard of, with a name you'll never be able to pronounce."

Fair enough. "What made you come here?"

"My father was...let's call him a judge, though not in the general sense. He was never elected, nor appointed to his position. He merely woke up one day and claimed it for himself."

"Oh?" I'm simultaneously riveted and repulsed by his tone. He doesn't speak of his father the way I speak of mine—Heyworth Thorne, anyway. There's no love lost or hostility spared. No hero worship.

"Some might consider my old home less than conventional," he adds, leaving it at that.

Which is an understatement if whatever he experienced forced him to blind himself at the age of nineteen. I'm tempted to ask, but I can take a hint. He won't hold back, and what he might say could disturb more than my appetite.

Changing gears, I decide to ask a far more pertinent question. "How long have you been watching me?"

"Now be specific, Ms. Thorne. Do you want to know how long I've been aware of your existence or just how long I've taken a *personal* interest in your welfare?"

I suck in a breath. His tone dipped just one octave above the danger zone. "B-both."

"A little over four years."

"After your brother's first appeal."

If he's surprised that I choose to divulge that bit of information now, he doesn't show it. He's stone again, completely unreadable. Though not quite...

I close my eyes and brace my palms flat against the table. Strange. He reveals more to me in darkness than I'm comfortable deciphering. Tension resonates from his end. His hand is braced against the wooden surface and vibrates ever so slightly, indiscernible to the naked eye.

"So you remember now," he says.

"That's why you hate my father," I admit, opening my eyes. "Because of Mathias. Isn't it?"

He inhales deeply as if just hearing the name stings. "A better man than Heyworth Thorne would have handled things differently. With Mathias. And with you."

But how? I'm not brave enough to ask out loud. Instead, I pose a different question. "What was he like, your brother?"

"Human," Damien replies. "A particularly decent one, but human nonetheless."

"And..." I swallow hard to gather up the nerve to broach this topic. "You think he's innocent?"

"I know he was." The grit in his tone warns me to back off. Discuss something else.

So I pick the obvious route of questioning. "So how did...*do* you plan to use me against my father? I'm sure you know all about the press conference tomorrow. I bet you have some brilliant masterplan to derail it."

I expect dramatics. Laughter. Or for him to throw his head back and announce some villainous plan so evil that I'll quake in my heels.

"How to use you? I don't know," he admits, each word sounding as though he had to rip it from his throat. "Expose you? Corrupt you? Your fate presents an interesting conundrum."

"How so?"

"Well..." He tilts his head thoughtfully and shrugs. "I can't decide whether or not your disgrace or your death would matter in the end."

Honesty. That's what he promised. I tell myself that as horror descends like a punch to the stomach. He promised me cruel, bone-chilling honesty.

"Y-you've thought about killing me?"

"I have once," he replies, his tone level. "The way I'm sure you've fantasized about destroying all of those who have wronged you."

"Punching, maybe," I rasp. "Not murder."

His cold laugh undercuts the intensity in his tone. "You may lie, but we both know the truth."

"So why haven't you killed me, then?"

"Therein lies the dilemma, Ms. Thorne."

Coming from a normal man, those words would be the punchline to a terrible joke. I could choke out a *haha*, throw my drink in his face, and storm away. I wouldn't be driven to dissect his answer into a million tiny pieces. One of them being: Did his supposed change of heart come before or after he met me in person?

"This has been very...illuminating, Mr. Villa." I flex my fingers against the table, though I'm not sure if I intend to stand.

His hand captures mine before I can decide, pinning it flat with the barest amount of pressure. "*Sí*. I'm glad, Ms. Thorne. Now, I would like you to extend the same favor, *por favor*."

The amount of patience he's shown tonight has me worried. What could he possibly want to know that four years of spying—a timeframe I'll stress over later—couldn't garner him? Nothing good.

"Fine. Ask away, Mr. Villa." I reach for a slice of pizza to disguise how my teeth are chattering with nerves. One impulsive bite later, I remember his murderous intentions. "Wait. You can ask me whatever you want *after* you prove this pizza isn't poisoned. Take a bite."

He doesn't move. A refusal? Not quite. He reaches into his pocket instead and withdraws a device too small to be a cell phone: his earpiece. "Bring a plate and silverware to my location, *gracias*," he snaps into it.

Damn. I'm suddenly aware of the grease on my fingers. What kind of man, no matter how polished, uses protocol for a slice of pizza? Then something clicks. No one even remotely familiar with Georgianos would ever show such disdain for it.

"You don't like pizza."

A muscle in his jaw jumps, a rare display of displeasure. "I've never tried it."

I wait for another punchline that never comes. In fact, he looks far too uncomfortable to be lying. He's tense: a mountain of man perched on a delicate wooden chair.

"Tell your slave to forget the silverware—"

"My men are family, not slaves," he insists. Quietly. Calmly. Even so, the tone conveys an unmistakable warning to never utter that word again.

"Your man, then. Tell your *man* to forget the silverware. Then give me your hands."

Now, it's his turn to look wary.

"We could sit here all night," I tell him, "or you can ask your questions before I get tired and go home. Now, I'm starving. Hands."

He raises the object to his mouth and mutters something in Spanish. Then he stows it and slams his hands onto the table. Pushing the box of pizza aside, I reach for one and bite back a swallow. I'll never get over how soft he feels. Perhaps our surroundings have something to do with it. His fingers are petal-soft.

With my free hand, I heft a slice of pizza onto his palm. "Now, bring it to your mouth," I instruct, "and take a bite."

His lips move, murmuring something I can't understand. Spanish? One word stands out. *Amen.* A prayer?

I don't have the chance to reconcile the pious nature to his criminal one. He grimaces. His fingers flex against the crust as though he's unused to the texture and slow ooze of melted cheese. Unlike how he handles flowers, or maneuvering, or—admittedly—women's bodies, I suspect pizza is something he's never been subjected to before. He's never seen it.

"It's shaped like a triangle," I explain. My fingers curl around his, helping him guide the slice to his mouth.

His brow furrows at the teasing swipe of sauce and dough against his lip.

"Take a bite," I instruct.

He does, only to promptly set the slice onto the bare table while he chews. I sense that pizza will not be a returning item on the Villa menu. As he swallows, he fishes through his pocket for a handkerchief and dabs at his mouth.

"Heyworth Thorne used to have lunch from an expensive French café hand-delivered to him when he sat on the bench. I assume that *this*"—he nods toward the barely touched pizza—"was not a regular entree on your dining table growing up."

I start to correct him only to realize that he's right in a sense. Daddy had our cooks prepare family-style meals every night and a healthy breakfast in the morning. Pizza or cheap snacks were treats I typically sampled only at school occasions or birthday parties. Before I became a Thorne, however, stale crust eaten out of the box while surrounded by the smell of booze had been a daily occurrence.

"I ate it more often before I was adopted," I admit.

He nods. "When you were eight."

If he expects me to react to his knowledge of yet another intimate detail of my life, well… I don't.

"Ask your questions, Mr. Villa," I quip. "I'm getting tired." I yawn loudly for dramatic effect, but he hunches forward, like a wolf readying to go in for the kill.

"Are you a virgin, Ms. Thorne?"

I nearly choke on my next bite and wind up coughing. Calmly, Damien offers me his handkerchief as I sputter, my eyes streaming.

"What does that have to do with anything?"

"Answer the question."

"And if I am?"

A muscle in his jaw twitches, betraying his impatience. "I would prefer a yes or no answer."

"What made you ask that question anyway?"

His teeth audibly grind together. "You didn't…feel like other women I've been with. I'd also like to give you the benefit of the doubt by assuming that you aren't skilled enough in acting to have put on the performance that you did."

Performance? I'm not sure just which show he's referring to. When he drugged me? Or all those nights of taunting him through his bugs?

"Again, what if I am?"

"So that's a yes, then." He sits back in his chair and folds his hands before him. If anything, he doesn't look satisfied with the answer he stole. His chest rises and falls, betraying harsh, slowed breathing. I do believe I may have upset the stone-cold Mr. Villa. I just wish I knew how.

"I'm invoking my rule," I say, hating how my voice shakes. Damn him for making me feel even a shadow of self-consciousness. "Why the hell does it matter to you?"

He breathes in sharply. Exhales even more harshly. "Because I want to proposition...*propose* an exchange."

"An exchange for what?" I ask stupidly.

He frowns, and then it clicks. *Oh.*

He wants to take my virginity. I let my eyes close again, for longer this time. My head spins. A part of me assumes I misheard him, but no. He throws off anger like heat from a furnace, infuriated. Annoyed. At himself? As strange as it feels to consider, I don't sense that his rage is directed at me.

No bother, because I feel more than enough fury for both of us.

"So no wonder you 'apologized.' Have you decided to replace murder with rape?"

He's a more equally matched opponent when I can't see him. I'm forced to feel what my eyes overlook. The tension lacing his posture. The unease emanating from his end. Every forced breath he takes in his desperate quest to maintain control.

"I don't want to rape you," he snarls, sounding disgusted by the prospect. I open my eyes and find him scowling. "How should I put it in a way you might understand? I want to fuck you, Juliana. More specifically, I want use of your body, at my discretion."

He could have said, *"I want to shake your hand and be done with it,"* and I doubt his inflection would have changed any.

"Let me guess. You want to deflower me in some sick way of getting back at my father?" I push back from the table so violently that his pizza slice falls to the floor. "Have a good fucking night in the literal sense. I'm sure your right hand will make a nice substitute for me—"

"Sit down."

I don't. But I don't storm from the room, either. I wait, breath bated, shoulders squared, my body thrumming with more indignation, hate, rage, and shame than I have ever felt at one time.

"I don't want you because of your father," he snaps. "I could think of several much less taxing ways on my part to humiliate him."

He sounds far too stern for jokes. It's the truth. And I now feel a sudden urge to warn my father of the danger he's really in. First things first. "So then why?"

"The experience," he says, as if he's used to picking and choosing which life milestones to conquer on a whim. "I've never had a virgin."

I scoff at the word use. Had. "So, I'd be just another trophy in your collection?"

"I'm willing to abide by your terms." He doesn't bother denying it.

Ah. No wonder he's been so accommodating with dinner.

"Take your offer and shove it up your ass, Mr. Villa," I say sweetly. "My body isn't for sale. Though I have to commend you for being the first man I've ever met who was so disgustingly honest about only wanting to get into my pants."

"Don't play coy with me." He pushes back from the table as well but remains seated. "I was there, Ms. Thorne, when you kissed me—"

"You kissed *me*!"

"I felt you. I heard you, if you haven't forgotten your little display. And…"

I don't see him reach out until it's too late. He snatches my wrist, tugging me against him. My hands scramble for purchase over his shoulders, but he tugs harder, nearly forcing me onto his lap. His free hand cinches my waist with breathtaking familiarity. I'm trapped.

"I must remind you that I have a remarkable sense of smell."

I bite my lip, torn between slapping him again and running. Or both. I attempt to wrench my wrist free, but he doesn't let go. He doesn't tighten his grip, either, teasing me with a glimpse of freedom.

"What is that supposed to mean?"

Suddenly, his face is parallel to mine, which allows him to speak directly into my ear. "It means that I know when you're lying." He lets me go and I scramble away from him, smoothing the front of my gown with trembling fingers.

"Well, try this one on for size: Goodnight." I storm toward the main room of the greenhouse only to falter over the threshold. He hasn't moved from his chair. Maybe that little fact makes me brave enough to utter one last taunt. "Let's say I was interested in 'negotiating.' What would you offer in exchange?"

I'm ready for something truly wicked. An insult that will justify more than a slap. A kick between his legs. A punch. Something vile enough to warrant assaulting a blind man and ruining what little shred of gratitude I may feel toward him once and for all.

"It's simple," he says, sounding more than willing to take the bait. "I'd give you whatever you wanted."

"W-what?" I shake my head. No way I heard that right.

"I said, you could have whatever you wanted. Within my means, of course."

I force out a haughty laugh the likes of which would make Sharla from accounting proud. "So if I asked you to get on your knees and kiss Heyworth Thorne's feet, you would?"

"I'd consider it." He doesn't even cringe at the prospect. "Though there is no telling what I might do to him after fulfilling your request."

Fair enough. "What if I asked you to give me your fortune?"

He shrugs. "I've had nothing before."

I blink. "Your studio?"

"Property," he tells me the same way another man would say *plastic fork*. Referring to something easily disposed of and replaced.

"What if I asked you to paint me every night for the rest of my life?" I ask. Though he had already expressed a fleeting interest in shortening it.

"Really, Ms. Thorne, I would have thought you'd have some imagination."

"Oh, Mr. Villa, I'm afraid my imagination couldn't come close to a man so desperate to get laid that he'd..."

Do anything.

"Understand one thing about me, Ms. Thorne," he says, flattening his hands on each corresponding knee. "I know at least ten women within a block radius alone who I could call to, as you put it, 'get laid.' Sex isn't what I want from you."

I'm frowning. "Then what?"

"The same thing I was after when I met Daphne from Moscow. I was curious how her accent might sound when she orgasmed. In exchange, I paid to have her family relocated and supplied with the adequate documents. I wanted to experience a woman with age, hence I gave

Catarina from Madrid a quarter of a million dollars. Marnie from Kentucky had never experienced, as she put it, 'kink.' In exchange, I jumpstarted her career as a successful model in Italian vogue." He ticks them all off like accomplished chores. *Daphne. Catarina. Marnie.*

I know without having to ask that each starred in a painting of his. One of them could be the figure hanging on my wall.

"Everything I do, I do for my art. Human nature cannot be copied. It must be experienced."

And, for some reason, he wants to "experience" me.

"I'm sure your previous ladies had a wonderful time, but I'm not for sale." My voice shakes, but damn it, I don't care.

"I do not purchase women." He sounds genuinely insulted by the idea. "Every encounter is a mutual one. And I can assure you that the curiosity went both ways. I'm sure you've thought the same thing, even in that sheltered head of yours. Can the blind man fuck?"

"Don't mock me," I hiss.

With equal vitriol, he says, "Don't underestimate me."

"You should take your own advice. Maybe I want my first time to be with a man who gives a damn about me, hmm? Have you considered that?"

A man who could understand my night terrors. Who could hold my hair when storms have made me vomit. Who wouldn't run at the mere mention of Simon.

It's a laundry list I stopped wishing for years ago. And I won't even consider how many boxes Damien has already check marked.

"A man who gives a damn," he repeats. "What about a man who gives a *dime*? My men earn a salary of no less than a grand per day."

And I spotted at least three watching over me. "Oh, congratulations!" I clap my hands. Thwack. Thwack. Thwack. "Give the man a medal! If you want to throw your money in my face, then fine. I'll send you a check to cover the expenses—"

"I don't expend my resources or time on people or things that hold no value to me." His tone resonates unlike any I've heard from him before now. Cold. Ice. Soulless. "You'd do best to remember that. I've taken an interest in your welfare, whether you like it or not."

"And *I* always honor my debts." Though I pray to any deity who will listen for the strength to forsake my pride now. "So ask your final question, Mr. Villa. I'm waiting."

From the set of his jaw, I know it will be devastating. Simon? Or something far more taboo, like the meaning behind that yearly bottle of wine? I feel every muscle in my body tense in anticipation.

I'm ready.

"I…" He sits forward, his head cocked. Then he stiffens. "Get out."

"W-what?"

He rises to his feet and advances toward me without warning. "Go."

"What are you—"

"Now!"

"*Con permiso*, brother." The voice of another man drifts through the glass walls of the greenhouse.

I turn and find a figure strolling down the main aisle, tall like Damien, with the same incredible bone structure. Only this man's eyes are fully intact, a haunting shade of amber, and his hair is closely cropped to his scalp. He's leaner as well, wearing a black shirt and jeans. Despite the casual attire, he holds himself with an air that rivals even Damien's swagger.

"I thought I should join you tonight and introduce myself." He turns that chilling gaze on me and smiles in a wicked display of white teeth. "*Buenas noches,* Juliana Thorne. I wondered when you would pay your respects."

EIGHTEEN

"*M*ateo." Damien pushes past me and nearly trips over the discarded pizza slice in his haste.

I've seen him angry, but never like this. His mouth flattens into a harsh line, stripped of emotion. It's how Daddy used to look whenever Danger, his prized mutt, ran out of the house off his leash.

"Whatever you want, we can discuss it later."

"There's nothing to discuss." Mateo shares the same light accent as his brother, but where Damien's words fall like haunting music, Mateo's are all sharp, thundering notes. He smiles and lowers his hand over his brother's shoulder, hard enough to jar his balance. "I merely wished to join you. I'm so lucky to have made it to dinner in time." His tone conceals a hard note that I sense is solely directed at Damien.

A warning.

"Pizza tonight?" He eyes the offering on the table and shrugs. "*Lo siento*. I'm being rude." He cuts his gaze to me: dark, cold eyes. "Ladies first."

"She's leaving," Damien warns. "Goodnight, Ms. Thorne—"

"Ah, but we have so much to discuss, Juliana and I." Mateo grabs my vacated chair by the back and deliberately angles it toward me. "Have a seat."

"Mateo," Damien warns through gritted teeth. Blind or not, his voice rings with an authority few men would ignore.

His brother laughs. "Oh, but I was so looking forward to our conversation," he says softly. "*Sí*. Who better to understand our recent troubles than another so-called murderer?"

Silence. It falls so thick that I can hear my heartbeat surging wildly beneath my skin. Like a tune composed of one haunting lyric: Murderer. Murderer. Murderer.

"Let's play a game. The life game." Smiling wide, Simon glanced from me to Leslie and back. "Who matters more?"

"*Sí*," Mateo says, sounding miles away. "If anyone could understand my predicament, it's this woman. A killer at the age of eight, self-professed, even—"

"Mateo!" Damien slams his hand against the table so hard that he knocks it off its axis.

I'm in the present again, stunned as what's left of the pizza lands on the floor.

Grinning, Mateo stoops for a piece and takes a bite. "It's no wonder she came calling," he adds after swallowing, "Did you want to know what it's like, hmm? To actually be punished for a crime?" He laughs and nods toward the half-eaten slice in his hand. "It's good. Much better than what they serve in prison. Plus, I don't have to stab a *pendejo* in the back for it—"

"Enough."

"I just want to know what it felt like," Mateo insists, his voice dripping with derision and charm. "To take away someone who mattered from a family who loved them. When you had nothing. No one. Though you did score yourself a rich daddy, eh?"

"I said *enough*."

"Oh, but we're having such a thrilling conversation. Aren't we, Juliana?"

"You." He pointed to me, grinning wide. "You pick. Remember the rules—"

"Juliana." Damien's voice has never sounded so cutting. It sinks into my skin, demanding my obedience. "Look at me."

I do. He's a blur, fading in and out of focus.

"This one matters, doesn't she? She's important, isn't she? She'll be missed, won't she?

"Watch." I had no choice.

He put the knife to Leslie's throat. Dug in hard enough to make her whimper. Then scream. And scream...

"Look at me!"

I blink and the flashback melds into Damien. Then the forest. Damien. The forest. Simon. Leslie.

A sound I vaguely recognize as coming from me fills the air. A wheezing gasp. Can't breathe. My fingers claw at my chest, but air won't go in.

Can't breathe!

"Enough!"

Warmth brushes my shoulder and I'm shoved toward the door.

"Go," someone commands.

"No." The second voice is harsher. "Let her stay."

I'm dragged another step forward. Another. Suddenly, the world sways and I'm pushed aside. I stumble against the wall, fixated on the scene unfolding before me.

Mateo grabs his brother's arm, his knuckles whitening over coiled muscle. "I said let the *puta* stay—"

Boom! In a flurry of motion, someone careens into a nearby planter, sending soil and crushed flowers sailing through the air. They groan, lying dazed in the aftermath. Thin. Mateo. His brother stands over him, his hands clenched into fists, his body radiating fury. *Madman*, Daddy called him. Now, I know why as his head swivels in my direction, his voice a slap.

"Go!"

My limbs jolt into motion. I run for the exit and across the roof without looking back. Panting, I reach the elevator and take it to the first floor. A man barges into the lobby at the exact moment the elevator doors open. I ready my hands to fight, my throat already clenching around a scream.

"It's all right," he says, crossing to me. His face looks familiar. Faint sound crackles from an earpiece he's wearing. "Mr. Villa sent me. I'm to take you home."

Home.

Where Simon's probably waiting for me. Where memories definitely are.

The home I don't deserve.

The life I stole by killing Leslie.

Damien's man hustles me onto the street, muttering something about a car being sent around. While he speaks, my eyes latch onto a yellow cab and I break away from him to flag it down.

"Wait!"

The guard can't catch up before I fling myself into the back seat and slam the door behind me. The bewildered driver watches me from the rearview mirror as I slap my hand against the back of his seat.

"Drive!"

Damien's man is already pawing at the door, but the cabbie doesn't need to be told twice. He plunges into the thick of traffic without waiting for a destination.

Not that I have one to give.

The driver refuses to take me beyond the city boundaries until I dial my accountant from his personal phone and have the man promise to pay a month's wages in exchange for taking me where I want to go.

A lonely stretch of road four hours away.

I make him drop me at a rest stop, where I attempt to buy a cheap bouquet of carnations before remembering I don't have a dime on me. Still, the cashier lets me have them out of pity, and I continue my pilgrimage on foot as the wind howls and nips at my hair and bared skin.

My flowers are frost-bitten when I finally reach a foreboding bend in a winding road. *Sorry, Leslie*, I mouth. They're not even her favorites, lilies. Just dying, pink petals and crumbling leaves.

It's so damn silent here, even now. Houses have sprung up close to this spot. There's a newer development in this part of town, a hint of civilization where there used to be nothing.

I don't have any trouble finding that small, dank crevice only a child could fit into. A matted layer of weeds has grown over the opening, remaining even as winter approaches. I perch my meager offering against a tree and then use both hands to tear the underbrush apart.

Twenty years later and it's never felt realer. Leslie's screams have never been louder. Simon has never felt closer.

I can hear him picking his way through the forest to find me and finish off the deed he taunted me with all those years ago. I hid here, holding my breath, shielded beneath a surging storm.

"You made the right choice," he told me then. *"You won't be missed like this one will be—"*

"Juliana!"

I jolt into awareness as reality makes itself known in varying degrees of pain. My burning, frostbitten skin. My cramping knees and my aching back. I'm hunched against the hillside, partially huddled within the crevice. Daylight stings my eyes as my ears catch footsteps prowling the woods nearby.

Fear grips my heart. Simon?

Whoever the figure is, he's persistent. "Juliana!"

Wait. I flinch. That voice doesn't belong here. Even the wind seems confused by his presence. It plays with the lilting notes of his accent, distorting them.

"Juliana! Answer me—"

"I'm here." My voice is a whisper promptly swallowed by the wind as I fixate on the imposing man wandering the woods just a few feet away.

He stops, his head cocked, sensing me regardless. "Where are you?"

I can't bring myself to move, even as he staggers within my reach, each step hesitant over uneven terrain. Somehow, he appears regal while tentatively feeling the space in front of him. He's still wearing his suit from dinner, a sauce stain along the lapel.

"Where?"

I stand slowly, biting a groan back. Is he here to finish the game his brother started? Or because of his stupid wager? Or because...

"Juliana, *por favor*. Where are you?"

"Here." I stagger toward him and grasp his outstretched hand in my own.

He's an inferno, clamping down like a vise. "You're freezing." The next instant, his coat is around my shoulders and he's shouting something into his headset.

"You...you found me?" I sound dazed. I *am* freezing. I don't have my coat, and frost glitters on my dress.

Damien says something else into his headset. Moments later, a man I recognize as Julio appears, panting by his employer's side.

"This way, sir."

For the first time, I realize that Damien literally went searching for me blind. He's unfamiliar with the landscape, using Julio's guidance to steer me forward. But his grip is sure and I'm so damn tired. When I lean against him, he doesn't even flinch. His arm slides around my shoulders instead, offering more support.

So strange. So surreal. Too fragile to question.

So I merely observe.

He and his guard came by car. It's parked along the road, and I'm guided into the back seat while the guard circles around to the driver's seat. Damien, on the other hand, takes the seat beside me. He says something to the driver in Spanish and the car begins to move.

I'm too busy shivering to pay attention to our surroundings. He could be taking me anywhere, for any purpose, yet I can't muster up the energy to care.

Though my silence, ironically, must worry him. "Don't sleep," he warns as if sensing my slowed, heavy breathing and how my eyelids drift lower by the second. "What the hell were you thinking?"

His anger sears my skin, hotter than the heat he orders the driver to turn up.

"Sorry," I murmur, unwilling to lift my head from his shoulder, even as I direct what little anger I feel his way. "It's not every day that I'm called a murderer to my face."

Recently, anyway.

I sense him stiffen.

"I…apologize."

And I *must* be delirious. My body reacts violently to the sudden warmth. My teeth chatter. I can't stop shaking, and the worse my tremors become, the more words in Spanish Damien snaps at his driver.

"*Vámonos!*"

The man must be used to the pressure, because he doesn't so much as flinch while maneuvering seamlessly through traffic. My old town flies by in a muted blur. The school where Leslie and I spent our last few hours of innocence. The old park. The library.

Nostalgia hits like a punch in the stomach. I squeeze my eyes shut against it and find myself sinking even further against the firm body serving as my sole support.

"No." His finger grazes my chin disapprovingly. "Stay awake."

"I'm fine." I grimace, but with a sigh, I peel my eyes open. His concern shouldn't affect me so much.

"Say something," he growls.

"My father's going to kill me."

The press conference is today. His big announcement. His triumphant return to the political sphere. All of it tarnished slightly by me.

"He delayed the press briefing," Damien says dryly. "It's later this evening."

"Good." A funny thought occurs to me. "How did you find me? Do you have me LoJacked?" Then again, the prospect isn't so funny.

"Julio followed you long enough to get the license plate of the cab," he explains. Not because he wants to, I suspect. He's stiff, resembling stone again.

I have a sudden urge to run my fingers along his jaw, testing the give of his flesh for myself. I do and frown. Soft like always, though he flinches at the contact. My fingers look like a stranger's. I've never been so pale.

"Why?" I croak.

"I have contacts who tracked your position out of the state," he adds without answering my last question. "Once I realized where you were headed, I knew where to find you."

"You were very thorough in your research, it seems." My fingers are still on his jaw. "Did you break into my old file?" I've been told the case has been declared indefinitely cold. "I guess you really do know everything."

"Not everything." Glowering, he removes his arm from around my shoulders and takes my hand, lowering it to my lap. But he doesn't let go. If anything, his fingers tighten as if he can force out the numbing chill through brute strength alone. "For example, I don't know what lasting damage you might experience from being in freezing temperatures for several hours wearing only a dress."

"You don't have to do this." But even as I watch his fingers intertwined with mine, I can't bring myself to pull away.

"New wager." His tone warns that, this time, there will be no negotiation. "Give me this one moment to give a damn about your welfare and tomorrow you can berate me all you'd like. *Por favor.*"

Apparently, he's not interested in receiving permission, because the car comes to a stop a heartbeat later. While the driver circles around to his side, Damien tightens his grip as if he's expecting me to resist.

But I don't. I allow him to steer me from the car and then through the halls of what I assume is a modest hotel, so unlike the posh, luxury high-rises we both frequent.

Julio enters our room first. He prowls the area, spitting out simple phrases all the while. "Bed at twelve o'clock, sir. Bathroom at three o'clock. Ten paces each way."

"Thank you," Damien says. Only now does he guide me inside, and I realize that this must be one of the many ways he navigates without his cane. "You can leave for the moment, Julio. See if you can have clothing brought for Ms. Thorne."

"Right away." Julio embarks on his mission while I'm marched into a modest bathroom.

Damien feels along the wall until he finds the light switch —for my benefit. Then he keeps going until his fingers brush the cool tile above the tub and then continue to the water fixture. "Remove your clothing," he commands as he switches the faucet on.

"I'm late," I realize as—of all things—my commitment to Daddy enters my mind. "My father's press conference. I've missed it—"

"It's been rescheduled," Damien says calmly. "Arrangements have been made. You don't need to worry about that now. What you do need to worry about is your internal body temperature." He gestures toward the tub. "Now, take off your clothing."

Memories of Simon must have stripped me of my free will. I'm an obedient little girl again, jumping to the rasp of a monster's growl. This one doesn't rest until I'm standing naked before him as he fills the tub to his preference.

Taking a step back, he nods to the water. "In."

My body rebels once I'm submerged in the deliciously warm bath. I can't move. I'm so damn tired—to the point where someone has to assist me when seconds pass without my cleaning myself. They hand me a washcloth, and then they wet it for me and drag it along my back and my shoulders. They work their fingers into my hair and lather it with shampoo. Finally, they dry me off into a towel and perch me on the ledge of the tub, apparently while waiting for Julio to bring me fresh clothing.

They stay. All without reminding me to smile, or hush, or be brave, charming Juliana.

I know they hear me crying, and they say nothing.

NINETEEN

I thought Daddy overreacted to the smallest crisis. Damien puts him to shame.

Heyworth Thorne could have found me neck-deep in a snowdrift, but I doubt he'd have his driver speed across state lines and all but drag me into my suite, where I find a private doctor waiting to examine me. It's a concern that borders upon...obsessive: a collector ensuring the objects in his possession remain unharmed—by anything *but* him.

I should resist.

Fight him off.

I shouldn't let him stay.

Damn Damien.

He waits in silence as the doctor pokes and prods me before declaring me healthy, though sleep-deprived and dehydrated.

"Primarily, you should get some rest," the man suggests, gathering up his supplies.

He's barely out the door before I find myself being manually steered into my room by a more formidable opponent.

"Wait..." I sway on my feet as Damien drags his fingers over my duvet and folds it back. "You don't have to stay—"

"You need to rest. At least for an hour. Especially if you are attending the briefing tonight. It will be starting soon."

"My father..." I groan, bracing my hand against my forehead. "He's probably called the FBI by now."

"Not quite." With a knowing tilt of his head, Damien proves he's outsmarted me yet again. "I had your building manager distract him with some lie about you losing your phone to explain why you're running late. You can arrive at his media blitz on time and he'll be none the wiser. Now, rest." He sounds so damn stern.

Not that I'm helping my case any; I can barely stay upright. I've never felt so drained. So exhausted. So vulnerable.

I can't ignore the subtle disgust tainting his tone—or the fact that he's trying his best to disguise it. For me.

"You want to tell me something," I blurt, sensing the truth in his tense posture. "About my father? Just say it. Please..."

"You need to rest."

"Just tell me." The desperation in my voice startles me. "That's why you've been so patient, right? To deliver the blow when I least expect it? I'm at rock bottom now, so just tell me now."

Of all reactions, he…flinches. "Juliana—"

"Are you going to have nudes of me plastered around city hall during the press conference?" The thought makes me shudder—but it's surprisingly low on the list of potential revenge plots. There are so many much worse. It's a dangerous game to play, jumping into the brain of a criminal mastermind. He already knows more than enough to decimate me. "Will you have my little recording play on the speakers? Tell me. I know you have something planned."

"And if I don't?" His tone cuts into me, sharp and demanding. *You think you know me, Ms. Thorne? Think again.* "What if my plan was far simpler?"

"What?" I ask. "If you truly give a damn about my 'welfare,' like you said, you'd just tell me—"

"What if I only had to tell you the truth? That your nightmares and your pain and the terror you feel at night could have been resolved years ago? That the man you worship hasn't done a damn thing to protect you. If anything, he's used you as a pawn in his own sick, twisted scheme meant to cover his tracks."

I swallow hard, hating the gruff earnest in his voice. It's harder to ignore than his usual smug mocking. "Like how?"

"All this time… You have no clue, do you? Think back to when he first adopted you, Juliana. Did you ever ask yourself why a man like him would take in a child like you? Why *your* case in particular drew the notice of such a cavalier defense attorney who rarely participated in even charity events?"

"Are you blaming my father for Leslie's death too?" I scoff. "Very funny."

But he isn't laughing. "Nothing could prevent what happened to you, except justice. Justice served to the man who hurt you before you could ever cross his path."

"The police never found him," I croak. "Does the all-knowing Damien claim to know his identity too?"

"What if I told you that you weren't the first or the second victim of this man. This killer? That several girls your age had suffered through a similar hell. Died. Mere shreds of evidence tied them to one suspect who escaped prosecution —not through fate, but intention?"

"What are you saying?"

"I'm saying, what if that monster had a damn good lawyer? A lawyer who got him off scot-free and had the records expunged so that the world would never even learn his name? A powerful man, with a powerful lawyer who allowed him to terrorize two little girls, killing one and leaving the other traumatized for life? Only after his mistake did that same lawyer adopt a victim of a crime he himself enabled and yet pretended to have suddenly grown a heart? A lawyer who likes to think himself a beacon of all things just."

His words create an invisible noose that wraps around my throat, tightening by the second. "No..."

"Should I be blunter?" Damien wonders, cocking his head. "What if that lawyer's name was Heyworth Thorne, and that everything he claimed to believe in was a lie?"

"You're lying."

"No. He has been lying. To you, most likely since the day he came into your life. It wasn't an act of goodwill that led him to you, Juliana. It was guilt. But guilt that hasn't led him to do the right thing and name your tormentor, even after all these years. He knows his name. He's known all along—"

"Stop."

"Why else erase the records?" He sounds so calm, though it feels like he's shouting. "Why else suddenly take an interest in supposed 'justice'? Heyworth Thorne never loved you. He merely used you like a trophy to assuage his own fucking conscience—"

"Stop!" Tears spray down my cheeks like bullets as I scramble to my feet and stagger toward the door. "You're lying!"

"Juliana, wait—"

"Leave me alone!" I'm running, escaping into the hall without bothering with a coat or shoes. Downstairs a car is waiting as promised, but when I enter it, I break.

Because I know that Damien wasn't lying.

If he could turn me against my father, he'd have everything to gain.

But Heyworth Thorne has a lot more to lose.

Enough that he'd use me as a pawn to keep it all.

*T*own Hall sits within a maze of reporters jostling for the right vantage point to cover my father's moment of triumph. It's a buzz of activity I quickly adjusted to while growing up in the Thorne family. From the age of eight, I learned how to smile on cue and nod solemnly when asked to explain how grateful I was to my father for adopting me.

When all along…

He might have known the identity of the specter haunting my nightmares. And all this time, he's said nothing.

Could such a man really be deserving of all the hate Damien feels toward him? Could he have allowed prejudice to cloud his judgment in the case of Mathias Villa?

The answer makes my stomach churn. Deep down, maybe I've known it all along: yes.

Heyworth Thorne is human—and I've learned the hard way that every human, at their core, has the potential to become a monster.

"Where to, miss?" the driver inquires, which makes me jump.

"H-here." I exit the car a block away from the press queue and spot my father amid a crowd of assistants near the entrance to the sprawling, Romanesque town hall building. It's a ritual of his: show up early, prep his speech, and ensure that all optics are picture-perfect.

My heart throbs as I observe him and try to see the man most of the world has turned against. His gray, balding head. His warm, gentle smile that eased my fear when I needed comfort the most. I try my best to strip away twenty years of loving Heyworth Thorne.

But all I see is an old man preening for the cameras, desperate to salvage the one thing he's cherished above all: his career.

I don't even realize I've slipped through the throng of onlookers until he spots me from the top of the steps, still smiling in his charming way.

"Sweet pea…" He frowns, looking me over. I'm in pajamas, my hair a mess, my eyes bloodshot. This isn't the perfect daughter he envisioned parading around today. "Didn't you receive the dress?"

"Why?" It's the only word I can get out as cameras flash and reporters shout questions. "Why did you lie to me? Why?"

"Juliana—"

"They said I was a liar. All the papers. The people. My own parents didn't want me because they thought I was…" I can't even say it. *A murderer.* "And you lied to me. Tell me he wasn't one of your cases. Tell me that you didn't know—"

"What on Earth are you talking about?" Diane asks, placing her hand on my arm. Beside her, Heyworth Thorne just stares at me, his eyes wide. "Darling?"

"Was taking me in some kind of pity party? A way to assuage your guilt? Or was it pride? Was that all I was to you?" I demand of them both. "All I am to you? A trophy?"

"Juliana." Daddy blinks, reassembling his mask. How ironic. He used to punish those who hide behind lies, but that's all he's ever done around me. "We need to discuss this in private—"

"No!" I turn, my eyes streaming as I scan the crowd for an out, any outlet. I find one in darkness: a sleek black vehicle with a hand beckoning from the back seat. Of all the things to fear, relief shatters the pain ripping through me—and I cling to it like hell.

"Juliana!"

I push through the throng of spectators and climb into the car. Black leather upholstery makes for a chilling escape. So does the man seated beside me.

"Drive," Damien commands, and I don't give a damn where he takes me.

Just somewhere far from here.

TWENTY

"Have you known all along?" I demand as the car melds into the thick of traffic. "That my father defended him? Leslie's killer? Do you know his name? Who was he?"

Damien says nothing. Too busy savoring the moment? Fine. I'll give him plenty to gloat over. My tears continue to fall unabated. I don't even try disguising the sobs ripping from me one after the other. "Who was he? I... I could press charges. Testify against him. Do something."

I try to picture him. Simon. My father and Simon. Could Heyworth Thorne have known more about the attack on me than he let on? No. Even thinking as much triggers a wave of bile up my throat that I have to choke down.

But the sinking thoughts nibble away at what little sanity I have left.

All those years of Simon's presents. Perhaps the man wasn't as omniscient as he appeared—maybe my father let him in. Let him taunt me with those memories. Could the home I'd thought was a haven have been little more than a kennel, with me as the pet, locked inside for others' amusement?

"I don't know his identity," Damien says, sounding eerily calm, no glee to be found. "I merely discovered the inconsistencies in Thorne's prior cases. But the records were expertly expunged and I never learned a name. I will say that only a powerful man could ensure that. Someone in politics most likely—"

"He never stopped after that night," I admit, my voice breaking. "S-Simon—that's what I call him. Simon. Every fucking year, on my birthday, he taunts me with the same fucking 'presents.' Like the doll, and the rose, and the ribbon. It's so I won't forget. He's still out there."

The silence greeting my confession is too much, too thick. Desperate to shatter it, I keep talking. "He made us play a game, you see. I had to pick. Who he was going to kill. We were near the woods. Leslie and I were walking home after I got jealous of her stupid doll and..."

We fell into a madman's trap.

I close my eyes as the memory threatens to unfold. For the first time in so damn long, I don't resist it. I *let* myself see the forest. Smell the blood. I can taste the fear, so thick and real...

"He made me pick which one of us would live or die. My rich, pretty, popular friend or me, the poor, pathetic pauper? And I..."

"You don't need to tell me this," he says. His accent dips in an unfamiliar way. Horror? Disgust?

Confused, I look up and find his jaw clenched, his posture tense. Men like him don't like to get their hands dirty after all. Not even figuratively.

But I can't stop.

"I-I picked *me*. I picked me," I repeat, choking out the secret I've suffocated on all this time. "I wasn't important. I wouldn't be missed. He *told* me. And he stabbed Leslie anyway! He…he stabbed—"

"Enough."

"He killed her," I whisper in defiance. "And he's hunted me everywhere I've gone ever since. So that I will never forget. My life is worthless.…"

And all along, Heyworth Thorne might have known his identity. Yet I wasn't worth bringing that monster to justice. I wasn't worth justice.

"You win, I guess," I quip, laughing at the irony. "I never want to see Heyworth Thorne again. Does that make you happy?"

"You still sound weak," Damien says, ignoring my question entirely.

I look beyond the windows and realize his driver has pulled up before the private entrance of the Lariat. There are no reporters lying in wait, surprisingly. Through his doing, I suspect.

"You need sleep—"

"Don't pretend like you care." My hand shakes as I wrestle for the door handle. "After all, this is what you wanted. To see the look on my father's face as my world fell apart—"

"You shouldn't be alone."

Damn him. He should be gloating. Smirking. Smug. But the stern tone of his voice robs me of my anger and all I can do is follow meekly as he takes the lead and escorts me inside.

His face reveals nothing once he's herded me into the elevator and we ascend to my suite. As we cross the threshold, guilt and gratitude feed off the potency of my fatigue. Only one thing can combat both: control.

"Fine," I hiss as he steers me into my bedroom. "We can play this game so that you can end this charade that you give a damn." In all honesty, the bastard's left me no choice after today. I have just one thing to leverage against him. "I'll agree. I'll do it."

He grabs my arm and pushes me firmly toward the mattress. "Do what?"

I climb beneath the sheets while he lurks there in utter silence. He's right: I'm exhausted. All at once, the gravity of everything slams down like a hammer. Delirium sets in, skewing my priorities. Heyworth Thorne and Simon are a million miles away. As my head sinks against my pillow, I watch him. His jaw has never looked so comparable to steel before. I bet he could crush diamonds with the weight of his scowl alone.

"Sleep with you," I say. "Now you can hold something over my father's head, like you've dreamed—"

"You're delirious," he says with obvious restraint. *Therefore, I'll ignore the fact that you're mocking me.*

"I'm serious." Am I? Maybe. The thoughts in my head all feel slurred and run together, but oddly enough, one seems startlingly clear. "I'll let you have my virginity."

He frowns and starts for the door. "Get some rest, Ms. Thorne."

"In exchange—"

His footsteps falter.

"I want you to…"

"Yes?"

The grated word makes me realize that I've trailed off, lost in my thoughts. I want more from Damien than a smart woman should. Small things. Stupid things. Tiny, inconsequential things that suddenly appeal to me more than any couture gown or high-rise apartment would. Maybe because I know deep down he'll never let me have them.

"I want you to find out who Simon is. I…I want justice." That elusive thing Heyworth Thorne spent his entire life promising to deliver. "Is that a fair enough trade?"

"I can give you that," he says quietly, as if it really is that simple. The powerful Damien Villa can do anything. So why stop there?

"And," I add, "I want you to stay with me. Until my birthday, anyway."

"Stay with you."

"In theory," I reply, murmuring.

"For a year?"

I can't tell if he believes me or not. To him a year must be a lifetime. For me, it's merely a brief lull before a recurring nightmare. "Yes."

"And I would stay with you?"

Suddenly, my eyelids weigh an unbearable amount and I let them drift shut. "It shouldn't be hard." Ironically, considering this is the price I'm naming for my body. "Send me fresh flowers every day. Stay with me when it storms. I'll even let you stalk me if you have to. Keep me away from my father if that's what you want. Just…"

"What?"

I almost forgot he was there, listening avidly to my slurred, disjointed wish list. "Just pretend that you actually give a damn… Pretend you want to keep me."

Maybe then I'll stop hearing Simon's voice slithering inside my skull: *This one will be missed. This one matters.*

You made the right choice…

And I'll never let you forget it.

For the second day in a row, I wake up only to be bombarded by a million chilling realizations. One, I'm not wearing my own clothing. Soft cotton has taken the place of tailored silk.

Two, someone tucked me into bed, drawing the blankets over me with unnerving care.

Thirdly, and most confusing of all, I'm alone.

My breathing echoes loudly in the silence as I peel my eyes open to yet another overcast, stormy-gray sky. I'm not worried. Gritting my teeth, I climb out of bed and strip the gray pajama set someone dressed me in. I'm partially within a trademark black-pantsuit ensemble when I hear it.

A man's voice.

The sound comes from my living room: a speaker rapidly communicating in a mixture of English and what I suspect to be Spanish. From his tone alone, I can tell he's in the middle of what he seems to do best: dishing out orders.

Partly convinced it's all a figment of my imagination, I leave my room half-dressed, only to be faced with a furious Damien pacing before my coveted view.

He must carry around impeccable suits wherever he goes. Today, his outfit of choice is gray with a muted tie in a similar hue. The moment I step closer, his head swivels in my direction. "Find him," he snarls into a cell phone before shoving it into his pocket. "You're awake," he says gruffly.

I swallow hard, surprised to find my throat dry and my lips cracked. "You're still here." My tone inflects at the last second, turning the statement into a whispered question. *Why?*

"How do you feel?"

Exhaustion robs me of my usual filter. "Tired," I admit. "I'm thirsty. Starving—"

"Side effects of hypothermia," he interjects in a fittingly icy tone. "I'll have something brought up."

Before I can blink, the phone is at his ear and he's snarling even more phrases in Spanish.

A glance beyond him reveals that he's been busy. My couch looks as though a man roughly the size of Damien has occupied it for quite some time—God forbid slept on it. A nondescript stainless-steel mug rests on my coffee table. One sniff and I can tell the blend isn't mine but the concoction of someone who prefers their caffeine black.

Do I dare believe he slept here overnight? Of course not. That would mean assuming he considered taking me up on my offer—and I already have an *I was just delirious and joking, obviously,* quip poised on the tip of my tongue. Seconds pass, but it never leaves my throat.

"You didn't have to stay."

He pauses in his solitary march, facing the view from the windows. Even though I know he can't see the dreary clouds through a jungle of concrete, his posture stiffens.

"I apologize again for the other day," he says, leaving me scrambling to wonder which night he referred to. "That was not my intention. For you to learn the truth in that way."

"I can believe that," I say. A man like him would have envisioned something far more devastating than a woman's minor mental breakdown in front of a throng of reporters.

In fact…

I know deep down it could have been so much worse. "I'm surprised my father hasn't come by or called…"

The subtle tensing of his jaw makes me suspect that he may have something to do with that fact.

"I don't want to see him," I admit before he can voice an excuse. "Not now. I-I can't…"

His lips part, but the door opens at the same time and Julio strolls in as boldly as if he lives here. He places a steaming cup of commercial coffee and a white takeout box on my counter. He nods to me and greets Damien out loud. "Sir."

Then he leaves, and Damien decides that taking charge of my welfare would punish me more than any comeback could.

"Eat," he commands, stressing the word.

I'd refuse if I weren't so hungry. My stomach growls as I cross over to the food and lift the lid of the container. The meal certainly isn't fare comparable to pizza. The buttered croissant and blueberry jam taste both heavenly and suspicious. Could they be a peace offering?

Looking at the man, I can't tell. He almost seamlessly blends into the background of the stormy city landscape. Sharp, harsh edges and sleek lines with streaks of odd light where there shouldn't be any. Like the fact that I can tell— whether on my couch or not—he hasn't slept much. The lines around his mouth are more pronounced than usual. He looks weathered and weary.

Because of me?

"I can pay you for the doctor's visit," I suggest. "And the gas you spent to—"

"I don't want money from you."

"Oh, that's right," I say softly. "You want my virginity."

I was wrong before in thinking that mentioning Mateo had triggered the worst of his anger. Sorely mistaken. This cold, silent creature, with his head dangerously cocked to the side, is Damien at his most volatile. My, how the man hates being mocked.

And in this moment, I'm poised to deliver the most crushing comeback I can and save face once and for all. Because I remember in cruel, crystal-clear detail everything I said to him. The price I deliriously dreamt up for myself. *Stay with me. Be with me. Pretend for me.*

Most pathetic of all: *Keep me.*

"Well?" I croak after choking down the last bite of my breakfast. "Have you considered my terms?"

I don't know which one of us is more shocked. My knees knock together. I feel liable to melt into a puddle on the floor.

And Damien looks like the definition of a man caught stepping on a landmine. "You remember?" His tone betrays more than mere caution. It's deadly.

"I require a yes or no answer, Mr. Villa." My God, how do I sound so calm? So in control when I feel anything but? "Did you find my terms agreeable?"

Of course he didn't. And his silence proves it. Without warning, he heads for the door.

"I have business to attend to," he tells me while straightening the sleeves of his perfectly crisp jacket. "It may take the rest of the day."

I still expect a direct refusal. Or for him to laugh and utter some parting cheap shot. Not to leave, shutting the door behind him. I can hear his footsteps retreat down the hall as my words hang on the air, sounding less calm the more I think on it and more…desperate.

Have you considered my terms?

No wonder he sounded so surprised that I'd mention them. He hoped I'd forgotten. Apparently, he wasn't willing to pay any price after all.

Bastard. My fingers tighten around the cup of coffee and I wind up throwing it across the room. It strikes my wall with a thud, splattering brown liquid over the industrial gray surface. Who needs Damien when I can create my own fucking art?

"Miss?"

I flinch as the accented voice accompanies a knock on my door. "Y-yes? Um…come in."

The door opens to reveal Julio, his expression stern—which makes the fact that he's holding a delicate vase of flowers in his hands even more comical and chilling. "Where would you like these, miss?"

Son of a bitch. I blink and find myself staring at the vase in a daze. The container itself is silver. From it sprouts a single black orchid with a telltale dash of pink across its center.

It's one of *his*, ripped right from the oh-so-private collection. I recognize the shape. The smell. The jagged stalk missing a single bloom.

By some miracle, I manage to point to the counter, and Julio obeys my silent command before leaving again, presumably to take up his post in the hallway.

Swallowing hard, I observe the petals of the bloom up close. It could be some sick version of a goodbye message or a threat. I'm almost content with that scenario.

But then I remember my own slurred, incoherent words.

Send me flowers every day.

Only a man like Damien Villa could make such a gesture feel like a warning.

~ The Duet Continues in A Taste like Sin ~

A WORD FROM THE AUTHOR

Hey there!

Thank you so much for reading! If you enjoyed the story, please leave a review and recommend the book to any friend you think would love this twisted world. You'd have my eternal gratitude. Even a short sentence goes a long way!

Then, come join the rest of us dark romance lovers in my Facebook Group where you can get snippets, sneak peeks of upcoming books and even help vote on aspects of future novels.

Come to the dark side:
https://www.facebook.com/groups/lanasbeautifulmonsters/

WANT MORE STUFF TO READ?
Join my newsletter and get a **free book**! Plus, you get to stay updated with any new releases, random giveaways and exclusive sneak peeks!
https://www.lanaskybooks.com/newsletter

Other Novels: https://lanaskybooks.com/

FREE BOOK - JOIN MY NEWSLETTER

DARK, TWISTED ROMANCE

Join my newsletter and get a **free book**! Plus, you get to
stay updated with any new releases, random giveaways and
exclusive sneak peeks!

https://www.lanaskybooks.com/newsletter

ABOUT THE AUTHOR

Lana Sky is a reclusive writer in the United States who spends most of her time daydreaming about complex male characters and parenting her Cockapoo Joey. She writes dark, twisted romance across several genres. Her titles include everything from mafia romance to vampires.

facebook.com/AuthorLanaSky

twitter.com/lanasky101

amazon.com/author/lanasky

pinterest.com/lanasky101

goodreads.com/lanasky

instagram.com/lanasky101

bookbub.com/authors/lana-sky

ALSO BY LANA SKY

For more titles by Lana Sky, please visit:

https://www.lanaskybooks.com

www.ingramcontent.com/pod-product-compliance
Lightning Source LLC
Chambersburg PA
CBHW071727190726
48292CB00003B/640